CAPTAIN

BLACK OPS MMA BOOK 3

D.M. DAVIS

CAPTAIN
Black Ops MMA Series by D.M. DAVIS

ISBN: 978-1-7354490-4-3

Published by D.M. DAVIS

www.dmckdavis.com
Cover Design by D.M. DAVIS
Cover Photo by DepositPhotos
Editing by Tamara Mataya
Proofreading by Mountains Wanted Publishing & Indie Author Services
Formatting by Champagne Book Design

This book is a work of fiction. Names, characters, places, and incidents are either the product of the author's imagination or are used fictitiously.

The octagonal competition mat and fenced-in design are registered trademarks and/or trade dress of Zuffa, LLC.

This story contains mature themes, strong language, and sexual situations. It is intended for adult readers.

ABOUT THE BOOK

D.M. Davis' *CAPTAIN* is a heart-wrenching journey of forgiveness, second chances, and healing. This sexy contemporary romance is Book Three in the *Black Ops MMA* series.

**Sometimes you have to break to find the person
you were *meant* to be.**

CAP:

I'm a bastard by birth.

Heartless by choice.

Love abandoned me a long time ago. Good riddance.

I have my family-by-choice. I don't need more.

Until *she* crept in, sank in deep, latched on, and stayed.

She's as broken as the day is long.

Yet I can't resist the pull to get her in my bed, in my heart, piecing me back together—for she's not the only one broken.

CHER:

I'm over men.

Destruction and pain are all they bring.

Been there. Done that. Check please.

Yet there is one—so many years later—who looks at
me like I'm a goddess.

Who makes me feel like I have something to offer,
that I'm *exactly* who he wants.

**Can these two broken souls come together to
discover the broken have more pieces to love, or will
they pass on finding their forever love?**

NOTE TO READER

Dear Reader,

First off, thank you for picking **CAPTAIN** as your next read. I'm deeply grateful and appreciative, and for that reason I want to advise:

For maximum enjoyment, I suggest the *Black Ops MMA* Series be read in order to fully experience the world and the characters who inhabit it. Though each book is a standalone, they are integrated with subplots that carry through books 1-4.

Please start with NO MERCY, then ROWDY before diving into CAPTAIN.

XOXO,
Dana
(D.M. DAVIS)

PLAYLIST

Something in the Way She Moves by James Taylor

Whiskey and You by Chris Stapleton

Only Happy When It Rains by Garbage

Dreaming With a Broken Heart by John Mayer

Broken Hales by Chris Stapleton

Before You Go by Lewis Capaldi

Count On Me by Bruno Mars

Fire and Rain by James Taylor

Angel by Sarah McLachlan

Till We Ain't Strangers by Bon Jovi & LeAnn Rimes

Count Me In by Early Winters

Maybe I'm Amazed by Joe Cocker

Shameless by Billy Joel

Crazy On You by Heart

Cover Me Up by Morgan Wallen

Sugar Pie Honey Bunch by Kid Rock

I Shall Believe by Sheryl Crow

Blessed by Thomas Rhett

DEDICATION

For my Divas.

You fell in love with Gabriel and Rowdy in NO MERCY.

You fell harder for Rowdy in his book, ROWDY, and
saw Cap in a new light.

Now, I give you CAPTAIN and pray you love his story just as much.

CAPTAIN

BLACK OPS MMA BOOK 3

CHAPTER 1

JAMES "JIMMY" CAMERON DURANT

PAST

DAWN ARRIVES LIKE AN UNWELCOME GUEST, entirely too early and with more baggage than I care to deal with or have room for. The ache in my bones and the pounding in my head is familiar, though—welcomed even. It reminds me I'm still alive. At least on the outside.

As for the inside, I'm not too sure. The ache for Vera doesn't lessen despite the distance, time, and the way we left things.

Me, walking away like every step wasn't ripping my heart out one shredded piece at a time.

Her, on her knees, tears streaming down her unforgettable face, yelling, "You'll regret this, Jimmy. Mark my words, you'll regret the day you left me to your brother."

And damn if she isn't right. I regret leaving her every day, every second, every breath I've taken without her scent coating my air supply.

She knew. I was an idiot with dreams of being a Marine, escaping my shit life with my asshole half-brother who treated me like I was a waste of DNA—his mother's DNA, to be precise.

Groaning, I get to my feet, biting past the nausea threatening to make me puke up every bit of alcohol and food I've consumed in the last... I blink at the blurry clock on the wall... four hours. Damn, I'm hungover *and* still drunk. Who knew that was even possible?

Nothing and no one has ever fucked me up as much as Vera can—could—in both good and devastating ways. From the first time my hungry gaze landed on her, to her latest words, which happened to reach me last night in the form of a *Dear John* letter, she's owned my pitiful, broken ass.

Late. Her letter took weeks to find me. Now, I'm too fucking late to stop her, to tell her I made a mistake, tell her I was wrong.

So fucking wrong.

By now, she's married to my half-brother, Barrett.

She didn't even like the fucker. Well, she might have liked him, but she sure as fuck doesn't *love* him—not like she does—*did*—me. Not like I love her.

Christ, I'm a sad sack.

After reading her letter last night and nearly ripping my short hair from my head, I set out for a more satisfying means of destruction—my fists to Harbor's face.

Damn if every punch received didn't feel better than the ones I landed.

Harbor is always up for a fight. He and I are one and the same. We live for the fight, for the matches we get on our downtime, the scuffles we get into when the need arises.

I stumble to the shower, wince when I catch my reflection. Sarge is gonna be pissed when he sees my face. I've got a fight this weekend.

I'm working toward becoming a Marine Corps Martial Arts

Instructor. My superiors might not be too happy about my need for extracurricular *interactions*, but so far, they've looked the other way. I hope today's not the day my luck runs out.

It's all I've got. I've lost the girl. The girl who was never truly mine, but fuck if my heart isn't telling me otherwise.

Get a grip. She's just a girl. There's a million out there just like her.

Naw, not like her.

First love sucks.

Last love.

So much for joining the Marines to become the man worthy of her.

Lock those useless emotions down. No more of this love shit for me.

If I still have a heart, it's on permanent hiatus.

I'd rip it out if I could.

CHERYL "CHER" STONE
PAST

No one warns you. There are no life classes you take as a kid to prepare you for being an adult and the pressures of parenthood, especially when you're still a kid yourself when you become a mother.

Gabriel was born two weeks after my sixteenth birthday. I thought I was in love with the man who saved me from my father and his lewd, disgusting ways. Germain did save me from that hell. But at the time, I didn't comprehend I was simply trading the hell I knew for a hell I didn't.

It started off slow. Rough touches. Terse words. Little by little my husband ate away at all of my *selves*: self-confidence, self-preservation, self-defense. Soon it was my words he took, my fight, my hope, my joy.

He beat it out of me.

He fucked it out me.

He took, and took, and took.

Hollow, barely enough strength to stand, I swipe at my busted lip and watch as my now fifteen-year-old son escorts his father out of the house, but not before Gabriel beat Germain within a hair's breadth of death.

I'm sad he stopped. Germain deserves death at the hands of his children. If it can't be me, Gabriel will most definitely do. My little girl Reese couldn't hurt a fly.

For Gabriel's sake, I'm glad he stopped. I'd never let my boy go to jail. I'd take the blame.

I am to blame, after all.

Germain is in their lives because of me, because I'm too weak to kick him out. I believe my husband… His lies—I am nothing without him.

As Germain stumbles for his car with only the clothes on his back, the money in his wallet, and the keys Gabriel forced in his hand, a smidge of hope blooms.

I'd rather be nothing *without* him, than nothing *with* him.

My sweet girl is at my side, wrapping herself around me, holding me up. My Reese. Only twelve years old and entirely too wise in ways she should never be, having seen things she should never have seen.

I shudder at the memories. My sweet girl. What have I done?

I'm an utter failure. If I didn't make that clear, let me rectify that now. I've failed my kids as a mother, as a woman, as a role model for the type of woman Gabriel should hope to marry, and the woman Reese could hope to become. I'm none of those things. I'm less than nothing. Not because Germain reiterated my faults on a daily basis, but because I allowed it to happen.

It might have been forgivable—maybe even understandable—when I was sixteen, but now, at thirty-one, it's reprehensible.

"Mom?" My boy, who stands at over six feet tall, towers over my five-foot frame. "He'll never touch you again." His eyes cut to Reese before he sweeps me in his arms and carries me inside. "Never fucking again."

"Language," I manage around the knot in my throat. Gabriel has a mouth like a sailor, but who am I to try and mother him now? He's earned the right to cuss all he wants.

"Sorry." He sits me on the edge of my bed, speaking over his shoulder, "Baby girl, get Mom an icepack for her face." He touches my side, and I flinch. "And the bigger one for her ribs."

"I'm fine, Gabriel. No need to fuss." I push his hands away. This isn't my first rodeo, but it will be my last.

"It's my right as the man of the house." His blue eyes, identical to his sister's, flash with anger before they soften on his next words. "I should have kicked him out years ago."

Oh, my Gabriel. My avenging angel. Tears threaten. I force them down, patting his cheek as he helps me lie down. "That's not on you. I failed you. I should have—"

"Stop." The authority in his voice should surprise me, but my boy has had to grow up so fast. He's a man at fifteen. "You did the best you could, Mom. It's his fault. Everything he did wrong is on *him*. Not you."

My quiet girl hands me an icepack for my bruised and swollen face. "Thank you, Reese."

She only nods, her gaze darting around the room, her hands jammed deep in her hoodie. She doesn't like to come in here. Dark things have happened in this room—things she shouldn't know about.

"It's alright." I try not to flinch when she shies away from my touch. "Gabriel will take you to get some dinner." I suppress a groan when he places the larger icepack on my side. "I'm just going to rest for a while."

Then I'll make a plan. Figure out where we go from here.

Matching pairs of blue eyes watch me cautiously as I try to get comfortable. My babies should never have had to witness today, much less the last fifteen and twelve years of their lives.

I'll do better.

I'll *be* better.

"Go. I'm fine. Save me some food." I manage to hold back my tears until the door clicks behind them.

I wait until I hear them leave the house, then make my way to the bathroom and strip. I need the punishing spray of a cold shower, beating my failures into my brain, body, and spirit so I never forget them.

I make a promise I will keep or die trying.

Never again will I be weak or vulnerable enough for a man to lay a hand on my children… Or me.

Never. Again.

CHAPTER 2

CAP

PAST

ERVES AREN'T MY ENEMY TONIGHT. IT'S anger. I'm ready to explode or implode—I don't really care which. I want to hit something as much as I need to be hit. Tonight's my last match in the Marines. I'm hanging it up after this. My team is relying on me to win.

I just need to fight. I could give a fuck if I win.

Vera had a little girl this morning, her third child. They could have all been mine if I wasn't such a stubborn, stupid fuck. Too prideful to ask her to leave Barrett for me—or stop her from going to him in the first place. I've got a busted-up nose and a broke bank account to offer her. But my heart… My heart is still forever hers.

A baby girl.

She could've been mine. Part of the family we could have made together.

Damn, I need to hit something. Hard. On repeat.

Until I can't feel.

Until this ache in my chest is beat out of me or into someone else.

Until I can't remember the feel of Vera's body under mine and the sweet way she calls my name when she comes. Like she's begging me to never stop.

I'd never stop if only she'd take me back. Forgive me. Give *me* babies. A family.

"If I win, promise me, Harbor, you'll knock me the fuck out." I bounce and stretch my neck, loosening up my arms and shoulders.

"The fuck?" His incredulous tone does nothing to dissuade me.

"She had the baby. Vera," I clarify when he just stares at me. "She's a mother three times over."

"Motherfucker." He scrubs his face with his palms. "I can't believe after all this time, all these years, seeing her only a handful of times, you're still that lovestruck pup I met in basic." He punches my shoulder. "That must be some magical pussy, Cap."

Cap, Captain, that's me. I've been a Captain for a while now. I'd accepted with the intent of being a lifer, but lately…"I need this. I need to forget. If I'm still standing when this is over… You knock me the hell out."

He smirks. "Is that an order?"

"Do you need it to be, First Lieutenant?"

"Naw, I'm always happy to hit you. You know that."

"Good." I can breathe a little easier knowing how my night will end.

I'm not throwing my fight by any means, but now I don't have to worry about dealing with my emotions on a winner's high. Nothing is worse than the adrenaline crash topped with a broken heart wrapped in regret.

If I can't have kids with Vera, I don't want them with anyone.

"How'd you find out?" Harbor draws my attention, saving me from my darker thoughts.

"Barrett." I punch the wall hard, but not hard enough to inflict damage, just enough to sting. "The fucker couldn't resist gloating." I swing my arms, loosening up my shoulders. "I'm surprised he got through. First time he's ever reached out, and he got through on the first try." I sigh into the stifling mugginess that sticks to me like a second skin. "Fuck my life."

"Fuck him. Fuck her."

My growl at his disrespecting Vera only makes him laugh.

"Man, if she was half the woman you believe her to be, she would have fought for you." He slaps my left pec. I welcome the sting. "But she didn't. She crawled into your brother's bed the minute your plane left the ground. That's not the woman you want in your life. Screw it—never met one who wasn't waiting for something better to come along. Fuck her. Fuck them all." He shakes his head. "Your own brother."

"Half-brother," I bite. Barely even brothers in his mind. I didn't ask for our mother to cheat on his dad. I had nothing to do with it, yet I'm the one paying the price. Always the outsider. Looming over him and our mom like Gulliver and the Lilliputians. Never understanding why I was never good enough to be his brother—acknowledged as his family.

I didn't care that we didn't have the same father. I just wanted to play, hang out, be stupid to each other in the way brothers are. But, no, I was never good enough for Barrett or his friends. Instead, I was the target of their pranks. The butt of their jokes. The victim of his wrath. He'd do anything to hurt me, including marrying Vera. She was mine before she even knew who he was.

Does Barrett even love her, or has she only been a pawn for him to get to me?

"Even more reason to say good riddance. Let 'em have each other, Cap. You deserve better. He's only got half the same blood, genes you have. But I've no doubt he's nowhere near half the man you are."

The more he disses the people I used to consider family, the worse I feel. He means well, but he doesn't get it. I left Vera with no choice. No options but to move on or live a life of seeing me a few times a year, maybe less, maybe more, but no guarantees either way. Plus, I'm not the man I was. Any innocence I had when we lost our virginity to each other is long gone, washed out by time, blood, and sweat. The man I was when I promised her all my tomorrows vacated a long time ago. Heartbreak and war do that to a man. For better or worse, forever changed—I can never go home again.

When the bell sounds, I'm already bouncing on my feet, ready to pummel the poor asshole in front of me. He looks like he face-planted into a Mack truck. Not unusual for fighters to have busted-up noses, but man, this guy looks like a pug. He snorts like one too. Maybe if I focus my strikes on the side of his face, the front will pop back out. Either way, he's in for a world of hurt.

I come out swinging, a fury of strikes, a blur of rage. If I can't forget her, I'll knock it the fuck out of him. Or better yet, he'll knock it the fuck out of me.

It's two days before I see the light of day. Harbor kept his promise to make sure it was lights out after I won my fight. He did a little too good of a job. A concussion kept me off mission. My team left without me yesterday. No matter how much grumbling, groveling, or ass-kissing I did, my CO wasn't going against doctor's orders.

Fucking doctors. Pussies. All of them. They'd hold me back for a hangnail.

As it stands, the pounding in my skull has taken a back seat to the ache in my chest. The beating didn't do the trick. I'm not sure what will.

Time.

Jesus, I've got too much of that. Orders to remain off duty for another forty-eight hours have me crawling out of my skin. I've never been much for pacing or idle time. If I can't go on mission, can't fight or be hit, then there's only one thing to do.

Scanning the med tent, I find my target. He's a big motherfucker I've seen around, but he's not a part of my unit.

He staggers to his feet when he spots me coming, his hand abandoning its crutch to salute before he's even completely upright.

"At ease, soldier." I grip his arm as he begins to list to the side, his face beading with sweat and swiftly fading from beat-red to white as a sheet. "Sit before you fall over." Or faint.

"Sorry, sir," he grits as he finds his seat and still manages to get in a sloppy salute.

"No apologies needed. What's your name, Private?"

"Jonah Tate, sir."

As soon as he says it, I know who he is.

The determined Neanderthal tries to stand again to properly present himself.

"Jonah, sit your ass down." When he hesitates, I force him to sit and remain so with a hand on his shoulder. "That's an order," I bark, grumbling, "fuck," to myself when the pounding in my head retaliates for the effort.

"You okay, sir? Should I call for a doctor?"

"No. Fuck, no." I wave him off as I sit beside him, my eyes closed, breathing deeply until the hammer in my head eases.

"Head injury?"

"Yep."

Something cold is placed in my hand. "It's water, sir. Drink it slowly."

After a few tentative sips, I crack open an eye, blinking at him. "Shouldn't I be the one worrying over you?" I motion to his injured leg, now propped up in a chair in front of him.

He chuckles. "I'm not the one looking like he's about to lose his lunch."

My stomach rolls on that reminder. "Copy that."

With amenable silence, calming breaths, time passes with ease, regardless of how upset I am, how I feel physically or about my unit going on mission without me. I'd like to think they can't find their asses without my leadership, but I know that's not the case. My guys are a well-oiled machine. The mission will succeed if it is accomplishable at all.

"Your leg. What happened?" I'd rather focus on Jonah than on my state of unrest.

"IED took out two of my guys. Shrapnel shot through my leg. Clean. Like a bullet. I should be good to go soon." He's eager to please. Perhaps too eager.

"Don't rush it. Heal. Be one hundred percent before you think of coming back."

He frowns. "Come back?"

I motion to his shipping stateside orders sticking out of his duffel. Maybe he's hoping he won't actually be sent home. "When's your tour up?"

I can't hide my smile when he blushes. Don't see too many grown-ass Marines blush. "Ten days."

Yeah, he's not coming back. Or at least he shouldn't. "Didn't I see you fight not too long ago?" He's one of the best heavyweight boxers I've laid eyes on. Raw, undeniable skill.

His blush deepens. "You saw me?"

"Jonah 'The Whale' is hard to miss. You're a big mother…" I motion to his hands the size of my head. "Fists like steel, if I remember correctly."

"I heard about your match the other night. I caught you in action a few years ago. Impressive."

I point to my head. "Remind me of that when my head isn't threatening to explode at any minute."

His laugh is contagious. "Same." He winces when he tries to lift his leg. "I head home tomorrow." I'm not sure if he's actually sad about it or feigning sadness because he thinks that's what I want to hear—believe.

"Well, if you ever decide to switch from boxing to MMA, you look me up. I'll be in Vegas. I plan on starting my own gym when I'm stateside."

I hadn't said those words aloud. I've thought it over the last few years, coming closer and closer to making that decision. But seeing him, the fire in his eyes. I want to get back to what I love, and as much as I respect the men I serve with, the Marines don't hold that place of honor.

"Seriously?"

"Damn straight." I stand, clutching his hand. "Captain Jimmy Durant.

Vegas," I reiterate. "Hell, with an arm like yours, I'd love to have you as a trainer if you ever get tired of gettin' it in the ring." Straight up, he's a talent I'd sweep up in a heartbeat.

"I might just take you up on that, sir."

"Cap or Jimmy. No more sir."

"Yes, sir…err…Cap."

"Oohrah."

"Oohrah, Cap."

That night I'm woken up by my staff sergeant. Five of my men died completing their mission—the one I didn't go on—because I was a stupid, brokenhearted fuck over a girl and got myself injured. I wasn't there for them because I let my temper—my emotions—get the better of me. And now the world was worse because of the men who were no longer in it. Harbor was one of them. He's gone. Just like that.

Could I have saved them? Would me being there have made a difference? Or would I be dead too?

I'll never know.

It's time.

Time to get the fuck out.

CHAPTER 3

CHER

PAST

THE FRONT DOOR BANGS OPEN AND SHUT AS Gabriel stomps inside. Reese jerks at the kitchen table at the sound of her teenage brother coming home. My heart races, then trots as I gain control of my fear.

Freedom of the heart and spirit differ from physical freedom. I had no idea. I thought freedom from their father would mean freedom from all the damage he caused too. Unfortunately, the mental scars require more than just physical absence to heal. Muscle memory is difficult to overwrite, curb, retrain. It's constant soothing, reminding myself—my body—what was true of the past is no longer my present or my future.

Gabriel stills when he enters the kitchen, his gaze bouncing between his sister and me. "Fuck, I'm sorry."

He's a typical teenage boy, larger than life and louder than a herd of horses. He did nothing wrong.

I shake my head and wave him off, my voice lost in the tightness in my throat. I kiss his cheek instead, searching his eyes to find the truth of his day.

His shoulders relax. "I'm good, Mom. Cap and Coach have me tied up and sore as fuck, but I'm good." He stuffs a wad of bills in my hand, ignoring my attempts to return it to his pocket. "For groceries. Rent is covered." He places a Snickers in front of Reese and squeezes her shoulder before kissing the crown of her head and whispering, "I'm sorry I scared you, baby girl."

She squeezes his hand with a minute nod. My girl is as quiet as a mouse. Like mother, like daughter.

I shake off the thought. She's nothing like me, not by nature. *Nurture* turned my girl inward. I'm hoping time will release her—set her free.

I tuck some bills in my purse—the hard-earned money Gabriel makes working odd jobs for Captain James "Jimmy" Durant at the local MMA gym, where my boy is learning to fight like a pro, not street fight like he started out years ago. He wants to go legit. I want him to be happy and for him to be able to protect himself in every way I've failed.

I was initially leery of James' intentions, but he's proven to be a stand-up guy. His formidable demeanor and stature keep me at arm's length. I can't deny his raw charisma, but I have no room for men like Captain Durant... Or any man, really.

Working on dinner, my body slowly relaxes as the kids chat quietly at the kitchen table doing homework. To look at them, you'd never guess they weren't normal teenagers getting along better than most siblings. Gabriel is seventeen, and Reese is fourteen for a few more months. He treats her like the innocent princess she should have always been but never got to be because of her father. When she's with her brother, her fear falls by the wayside. She comes alive, beaming at him, eating up the attention he gives her. She's desperate for it.

No matter how much I want it, their relationship will never be normal—equal.

He will always be her protector.

She, his broken little sister.

He works hard to keep a home over our heads. I work, but it's never enough. I'm limited by my own demons keeping me locked in this kitchen, baking my heart out day in and day out to sell enough to keep us afloat with Gabriel's help.

Losing myself in creating something sweet for a change.

Someday I'll stop looking over my shoulder.

Someday I'll open my own bakery—storefront. Where people will come from near and far to eat my delicious treats they can't get enough of. The sweet smells of fresh bread and chocolate that now waft around my kitchen will lull them into my store. They won't be able to resist just a taste, a morsel, a treat from my kitchen to theirs. My redemption in every bite they take.

Someday I'll make it up to my children, be worthy of their love, and make amends for the past I was too weak to walk away from.

Someday I'll be whole again—we all will.

CHAPTER 4

CAP

PAST

I PUNCH OUT A BREATH AS MY CHEST SWELLS WITH pride. My Black Ops MMA gym, turned party central, is hosting Gabriel's going away party. He made it through Special Operations Combat Medics training and deploys tomorrow. The room is full of my fighters, staff, and their significant others—or hookups for the night.

We've become a family over the past few years, closer than I ever could have hoped. But none of them mean more to me than the tough-as-nails kid who came charging through my doors, barely fifteen, looking for a fight.

I provided that and more. I gave him direction, an outlet for his anger, a path for his restless heart. Now, years later, he's the most promising heavyweight contender I have. Yet he's chosen to put his fight aspirations on hold to serve his country and support his family—his mother and sister with guaranteed income, and training he can use once he leaves the military. Nothing could be nobler than that. Fuck if I'd ever let them starve, but it's his family, his decision. I've gotten him this far. The military will take him the rest of the way.

Nothing could make me prouder. Proud is a lackluster term for what I'm feeling. I imagine it's close to what a father feels for a son who's grown into a man of distinction, surpassing expectations. Gabriel "No Mercy" Stone has come a long way, and he's nowhere near done. The protector in me worries for his safety, knowing what it can be like, what he could be heading into. But I have faith in him, in his training, and his purpose to be more than a Special Ops Army medic. He'll come home.

He sure as fuck better.

"Hey, Cap." Jonah, one of my trainers and former heavyweight boxer I met in the Marines, clinks his beer with mine. "It's a nice turnout." He nods to the room. "Don't ya think?"

"Yeah, sure is." My gaze lands on the man of the hour, standing protectively over his sister and mother. "He's done good."

He comes from a piece of shit father, who, lucky for him, I've never met, and the painfully reserved woman at Gabriel's side. He watches the room, his gaze returning to Frankie time and time again. It's a good thing he's leaving. Frankie doesn't deserve his defensive MO of angry glares and biting words. She's the sweetest girl I've ever met. Similar shitty upbringing: ass of a father, no mother, left home to live with her current boyfriend Austin. He's nowhere near good enough for her. But I can't say Gabriel would be any better—at least not yet. Maybe someday. But until that day, I'll keep her close, and he'll leave to become the man he's supposed to be.

"I'm a..." My feet move before I can even complete the thought or think better of intruding on the Stone family's bubble. Not much gets past Gabriel when it comes to his mom and sister. Reese is still a kid in high school, quiet as a mouse. Cheryl, their mother, isn't known for saying much, but I swear I hear volumes when she looks at me.

"Cheryl, Reese, it's good to see you." I soften my natural growl. The last thing I want is to scare these two who mean the world to Gabriel and have survived more than most even know exist.

Reese offers a wisp of a smile before slipping into her brother's shadow. I hide my cringe. She's painfully shy and reserved. I pray someday, somehow, she finds her way in the world that scares the hell out of her. Cher isn't a great example when it comes to branching out—working from home too. Maybe Reese will find her inner Gabriel and come out kicking ass. Soon, I hope.

Cher clasps Reese's hand, keeping her daughter from escaping altogether. "James." Cher's eyes pierce me with their vivid blue, same as her kids', but richer in focus and wicked, silent communication skills. I've never met anyone who could say so much with so little. But this time, I'm graced with her sultry voice as she continues. I hold my breath, not wanting to miss a single word. "Thank you for hosting Gabriel's party. It's nice to see so many come to celebrate his achievements." Her pride is evident. Her discomfort is too.

I want every interaction between us to prove that everyone in the world doesn't mean her harm.

I've only known Cher for a few years, and in that time, she's shown herself to be a determined, reserved woman who's light on words and even tighter with emotions. Slowly, I've learned to read her. Now, it's hard to see the woman she used to be when every look, movement, word said or unsaid resonates inside me as if I can feel her in my bones.

It's disconcerting as fuck, given that I'm not a man open to romantic entanglements or nonphysical relationships with women. Except Frankie. She's the exception and always will be when it comes to opening my heart to a woman. She's more daughter than friend. If I were ever to have kids, I'd want them to be like her—or maybe even a son like Gabriel. As for the other fighters and staff, they're my family by choice, my brothers in arms. For most, military connections brought us together. For some, it's the broken misfit I recognize and relate to.

Gabriel clears his throat. His questioning brow has me stepping back.

I was staring—at his mom. That won't do.

"Let me know if I can get you anything," I say to Cher and Reese, then to Gabriel, "See me before you go, son."

"Yes, sir."

Making a hasty departure, I don't look back. I made my choice a long time ago. I didn't know at the time that leaving Vera to join the Marines would be a stake in the ground toward never getting married or having my own kids. I was fucking eighteen. What the hell did I know about forever that went beyond the tip of my own dick? Not a fucking thing. Life, on top of choices—both mine and hers—nailed my single man coffin shut. My surrogate children are the fighters I take under my wing. I know how to fight. I know how to protect. That's all I have to offer.

I can't be anything other than an arm's length protector to Cher and Reese. A guardian. A promise to Gabriel to look out for them while he's gone. I can't betray that trust by fucking his mother.

Christ. It's not like she'd have you, asshole.

Truth. Cher has no room in her heart for men. I can read that sign a mile away. Plus, I sure as fuck am not looking for a complicated hookup. And *everything* about Cher Stone screams complicated.

CHER

"Promise you'll be safe." I refuse to focus on the danger he could be facing. He's my baby. He'll always be my baby. I'll fret over him every day, but beyond a promise he may not have control over, I won't harp on it. It will do neither of us any good for me to worry over what I can't control. I hug Gabriel longer than he's comfortable with, but he's feeling generous and letting me have these extra few moments.

The Army only gave him four days' leave. Barely enough time to see him, dote on him, love him as best I can before he's off for another tour. This time as a Special Ops Medic in the Green Berets. I couldn't be prouder of him and the man he's becoming. He's far exceeded my every hope. He could have easily fallen into gangs and street fighting. James gave him the chance he needed to pull himself up, become more than he would have ever been on his own. Now the Army has given him a profession if his MMA dreams don't come true, but more than that, the Army gave him confidence to match his cockiness.

"Promise." He squeezes me tighter. "You too. No ragers. No crazy book club parties."

I stifle my chuckle. My son knows me too well. None of those things would ever happen. Though I do love a good book, I enjoy them in private. My social circle is small and has shrunk back to one—Reese—now that Gabriel is leaving. He's been my rock for so long after he unfairly became the man of the house. The past few years he's been away, we've learned to survive without him. I don't want him to leave again, but I'd never ask him to stay and give up his dreams and aspirations to dissuade my fear of being without him, or fear of losing him.

Of letting him out of sight where he can be hurt.

Then again, he got hurt when he was with me.

It's just a few more years, then he'll be home. For good.

With arms that don't want to release my firstborn, I step back. He needs to go. I bite back tears as he hugs his sister, whispering something to her that just makes her cry harder. He's been her protector, her security blanket for so long. I'm not sure how she—or I—will survive without him—again.

But we will. We must.

"If you need anything, you call Cap." His voice is rough with emotion.

I want to wipe the scowl from his brow, but he's earned the right to scowl at the world. I only pray he finds someone to remind him how to smile—someday.

"We won't—"

"If you do"—he grips my hand—"you call Cap. If it's an emergency, he'll know how to reach me." He kisses my cheek. "Promise. If you need anything—"

"Okay." I push at his chest, but the man is immovable. "I'll reach out to James if we need anything." Which we won't.

"Cap, Mom. Call him Cap."

"Pshh." I can't call that man Cap. It feels too personal, and also *im*-personal, and things with him already feel too… "James is respectful. He deserves my respect."

I can never pay him back for what he's done for Gabriel. He gave my son a safe place to vent his anger and turn it into a skill. Many may not believe in fighting for a living, but when you grow up like he did—like I did—you either learn to fight or get beaten. I fell on the latter spectrum. I'm proud of my son for always being the fighter. Yet, a part of him is a healer too. Thus, his medic training. I was the first person he cared for, tried to fix with his healing ways and his fists toward his father.

My big boy shakes his head, exasperated with me already.

"Go. You'll be late." I smile and blink through my tears, trying to get one last look at his beautiful face. My avenging angel.

One final hug between the three of us, then he closes the door behind him.

I can't follow. I can't watch him drive away. Instead, I nod to Reese, who follows me into the kitchen where my baking for the day awaits.

"How many today?" Her voice is tight with the strain of keeping her emotions in check.

I avert my gaze as she swipes at her eyes. If I see my girl crying, I'll start all over again. Instead of answering, I slide the list over to her and get to mixing the first cake. Behind me, Reese turns on the oven to pre-heat and gets to work helping me—as she always does, until it's time for her to leave for school.

The day moves by on automatic. Me, lost in my baking, freeing my mind from worrying over Gabriel, and forgetting to eat more times than not. It's crazy, but even though I'm cooking and in the kitchen all day—around food, I forget. The smells fill me up, I guess.

A knock at the door has me nearly jumping out of my skin before noticing the rumble in my tummy. One look at the clock has me sighing my relief as I wipe my hands on a kitchen towel and open the front door. "Hi, Tom."

"Hey, Mrs. Stone."

I don't bother correcting him. It's probably better he thinks I'm still a *Mrs.* than a *Ms.* Tom is a nice kid, a little too friendly for my taste, but he does a good job of delivering my desserts to the restaurant his dad owns in town.

He steps inside, following me to the kitchen where his order awaits. "Damn, it always smells so good in here. Someday I'm going to have you bake me a cake so I can have the whole thing to myself."

"You tell me what kind and when, and I'll have it ready for you."

I've got everything packed in boxes by the time he finishes a mini lemon curd tart. They'll add fresh berries before serving. But he doesn't seem to miss the berries one bit.

"It's so good. The perfect amount of sweet and tart." His cheeky smile gives me pause. "But it's your seven-layer chocolate fudge cake that gives me wet…" His eyes widen in shock.

I freeze, unsure of how he was planning on finishing that sentence. I imagine it was highly inappropriate, and nothing I care to hear from his lips.

"I'm sorry. I lost my head for a second. That's what your baking does to me." Avoiding eye contact, he picks up the first stack of boxes. "I'll just get these in the van and be back for the rest."

Relieved to be alone for the moment, I stack the boxes for his next load, ensuring his departure is sooner rather than later now that things feel… uncomfortable. He's a nice enough boy—man. He's eighteen now and recently had a growth spurt, taking him from gangly teen boy to not-as-safe-feeling almost-man. He's no stranger, but I prefer to keep to myself and not have people—men—in my space or in my home. Plus, the way he looked at me…

No, I'm imagining things. Germain. When will I ever be free of him?

As soon as he's gone, I clean up and start dinner. Reese will be home soon. I want her to have a good meal before she starts on her homework.

She works hard, dedicated to her studies, staying out of trouble. Fueling her body is the least I can do.

I hope someday I earn the right to be her mom. She's too sweet to be my daughter and entirely too damaged to not be.

Damn you, Germain, wherever you are. If you're not dead, I wish you're rotting in hell being tortured by all kinds of demons that make you feel like the trash you are.

On that treacherous thought, I slip the lasagna in the oven to bake until gooey and delicious. Then I start the cleanup and prep for tomorrow's orders.

CHAPTER 5

CAP

PAST

FOR YEARS I'VE STOPPED BY EVERY FEW WEEKS TO mow Cher's lawn while Gabriel has been away. Hell, even when he's home on leave for a week or two, I still do it. It's a calming, familiar routine. I won't say it's also a chance to catch a glimpse of the woman who's on my mind entirely too much with little to no encouragement—from me or her.

Usually that glimpse only came when she'd slip a bottled water out the door, sometimes a sandwich, or if I'm really lucky, a piece of her chocolate cake. That all changed a few months ago when she stepped outside and sat at the patio table, pouring *two* glasses of lemonade and placing a plate of barbeque brisket sandwiches on the table. She didn't say a word. She pulled out a book and read.

She continued to read as I slowly made my way over, wiping at my sweaty face and washing my hands inside with her small nod of approval. She read as I devoured the succulent meat, perfectly sweet and spicy, surrounded by warm fluffy bread that simply served as a tool to shovel the food in faster.

I didn't get a word out of her, but I felt like we had a meaningful conversation nonetheless. When I left with leftovers, cinnamon rolls, and a bottle of water, my head was still reeling from the change in behavior and also from the familiar pull of being right where I belonged. The companionable silence was soothing instead of deafening, peaceful instead of awkward, welcoming instead of off-putting.

As the coming weeks passed, our encounters were similar in nature. I'd mow. She'd make her way outside at some point with refreshments and food. Always the best damn food this Texas boy has ever tasted. I'd speak. She'd listen. She'd read, and I'd watch as her face and her body spoke volumes on what the words on the page were doing to her. She'd bite her lip, play with the edge of the page, and when she'd get to what I imagine was a particularly steamy part, she'd shift in her chair, flit her eyes closed for a second, taking a deep breath and letting it out slowly. It was mesmerizing—*she* was mesmerizing. And hot as hell.

But it was the silent tears that got me, made me want to rip that book out of her hands, pull her into my lap and soothe the sadness away with my words, my mouth, or any other part of me she'd allow near her, or God forbid, inside her.

I scrub my face at the memory. Fuck. Get. A. Grip.

She hasn't made an appearance today. Tom, the guy from the restaurant is here to pick up his desserts for the weekend. I don't like the guy. He's amenable enough, but there's just something off about him. He was a scrawny teen when I first met him. Now, he's a taller, thicker, early twenties restaurateur. He's never given me a reason to dislike him… And yet I do.

Jealousy over a kid getting to spend more time with Cher? That's not quite it either.

She works her ass off for him, baking double on Saturdays to cover his weekend demands. Sunday is the only day she takes off. But that extra baking and the douche in her kitchen is taking her away from noticing me.

I'm not pouting. I'm a grown-ass man. I don't pout. But I've been mowing for a while now, and usually she'd have stuck her head out to say hello at least.

Damn it, maybe I *am* jealous of a punk kid.

"Fucking Tom," I grumble, pushing around the side of the house to start on the backyard.

CHER

My gaze keeps skittering across the backyard as James mows my lawn, like he does every few weeks. Almost always on Fridays, but he didn't show yesterday, to my unwelcomed disappointment.

When the mower started up this morning, I felt like a schoolgirl before my father got his hands on me, before I was broken into unrecognizable pieces by Germain. For a few brief moments, I felt innocent, untouched, and eager for the oblivious man outside to notice me.

I all but ignored Tom while he was here—thank goodness he's young and self-absorbed as most boys are at that age and didn't notice my rudeness. His running diatribe on how much better the family restaurant is doing since he took over for his dad is all he can talk about. Plus, how much he loves my *sweets*. The way he says *sweets* makes my skin crawl. I'm sure he doesn't mean to, and I'm sure it's just me. I could be imagining it. But I'd swear over the years, his gaze has started to linger a little too long for me not to believe he's interested in more than just my edible sweets. He's just a kid. I cringe at the thought.

Legal or not, he's entirely too young for me to see him *that* way. Even if I hadn't known him since he was a child, he's Gabriel's age. But he isn't a kid anymore—he's grown into a young man with desires of his own. He should have his eye on Reese and not me. But as much as I don't want his attention, better me than my sweet girl. I may not be any more equipped to deal with it than her, but he's unlikely to damage me further. A broken vase is already useless.

Still, even after he's long gone, I'm shaky, off-kilter, untethered, and wholly unprepared for Cap when he knocks on the back door.

On my way to opening it, I swipe a kitchen towel, giving my hands something to hold on to 'cause, God knows, it can't be him I cling to.

The hit of the early afternoon heat when I open the door makes me feel horribly selfish for not bringing him a drink earlier. "James." I step back, waving him in.

"Afternoon, Cher." He eyes me cautiously as he washes his hands.

I turn away, getting him a drink. I can only take so much of James' focus before I start to crumble—and I'm not even sure it's in a good *swoony* way or a *I'll never be solid again* kind of way.

I set his drink on the kitchen table, motioning for him to sit. He does, drinking the whole glass of water. I refill it and place the pitcher of fresh lemonade on the table for him to switch to when he's ready.

My back to him, making him something to eat to occupy my trembling hands, I can still feel his heated gaze, but at least he can't see my unease full-on.

"You alright? Did Tom upset you?"

I bite the corner of my bottom lip but only shake my head. No, Tom didn't really do anything... It was the idea of what he *might* want from me. What he'll do if I say no. Not that he's even crossed a line, or even wants to! I'm being silly, crazy. If James only knew how often people upset me, he'd know for sure how fragile and incompetent I am.

His shadow creeps up over the counter, the only notification that he's on his feet and near. "Cher, you're obviously upset." His warm hand presses to the middle of my back. "Sit. Let me finish this. You've been baking all day. Take a breather."

If I thought arguing would do me any good, I would, but he wouldn't listen, and it would only serve to upset me. I'm not great at confrontation—it only ever made things worse for me—for the kids. Actually, I avoid it at all costs.

"Have you eaten?" His tone has me glancing at him over my shoulder before filling a glass of water for myself. I don't miss his frown when he catches the slight shake of my head. "You're a teeny thing, Cher. You can't afford to not eat."

He pulls another plate from the cabinet, making himself at home. Anyone besides Gabriel or Reese doing that would rub me the wrong way, but Cap is only being nice, making a plate for me too.

"When did you have time to make this?"

All I have is time. I point to the roaster he's serving up roasted chicken and vegetables from. I started it this morning after getting the first batch of strawberry pies in the oven.

I fidget with edge of my shirt. He shouldn't be waiting on me.

Oh no! I forgot napkins and silverware. Panicked, I jump to my feet, crashing into Cap, his hands full of food.

"Oh—" I scurry back. I've made it worse. I always make it worse. He was right about me. Germain was right. I'm useless. I deserve what comes next. "I'm sorry. Don't... I won't forget again. G—"

"Fuck, Cher." James' concerned frown has me sinking further into myself.

Oh, God. I swallow through rising bile.

He's not Germain. I'd been about to call him...

Stupid. Stupid. Stupid.

I can't believe I said that out loud—to *him.*

Way to seem stable and healthy, Cher.

Cap places our plates on the table and steps into me. "Cher, I won't hurt you." He holds his hands up, drawing closer. "I'd never hurt you."

Closer still, nearly touching, my heart races, and my downcast eyes prick with pending tears.

"I'm gonna hold you." His arms wrap around me, not yet touching my flesh. "Do you want me to?"

Silence is my only refuge, the one I've cherished, held entirely too dear for more years than I can remember. But right now, at this very moment, I wish I could scream, "Yes, please. Please hold me until I'm no longer scared and embarrassed," which would be for an eternity, for my life is one endless stream of fear and embarrassment, only the words are locked inside.

Even though he's holding without touching me, the heat radiating from his arms makes me want to cry and wallow inside. It feels like safety—relief.

And I can't speak through the feeling clogging my throat... Desire?

Then fear.

Familiar friend, fear.

What if he leaves without me experiencing what it's like in his arms? The incredible sense of loss that threatens to overtake me at the thought drowns the hesitation.

I manage the tiniest of nods.

His exhaled relief matches my own as he secures me in a hug like I've never experienced. Warm and safe, I burrow in. Shame should have me scurrying away. Yet all I can think is... Nothing, absolutely nothing.

The spinning wheel of worrisome thoughts stills.

The fear racing through my blood evaporates.

And the tightness in my lungs releases.

When I take a full, deep breath, so does he. His embrace tightens as he murmurs into my hair, "You're alright, Cher. I've got you."

Dear God, I wish you did.

Before I can embarrass myself by begging him to show me what else would be entirely different with him, I find my sanity and squirm out of his hold. Cool air surrounds me the second I separate from him, reminding me how cold and alone I am. I swipe at my face, dump my plate in the trash, and ignore his heedless protests behind me.

"I'm sorry," is all I can muster before escaping to my room.

CHAPTER 6

CAP

PAST

THE LAST TIME I WAS HERE, CHER WENT running to her room to escape me. I couldn't help staring at her lips when she pulled away from me. I wanted to kiss the uncertainty from her face. The raging hard-on in my pants was probably not helping her panic, I've no doubt.

I fucked up.

Something spooked her. She jumped from the table, ran smack dab into my chest and bounced off me faster than I could stop her. Panic and fear riddled her composure. Then she begged me not to hurt her. She didn't get the words out completely, but I *saw* it. She's an open book to me. She thought I was going to react like *him*. That *I* was going to punish her for whatever it was she said she wouldn't forget again.

I wanted to kill her ex nearly as bad as I needed to hold her and stop her racing thoughts, her fearful stance, and her associating *me* with that asshole who hurt her.

I didn't mean to get turned on—I wasn't even trying to go there. But she nuzzled in so good. As tiny as she is, she fit me just right and felt all kinds of womanly in my arms. She's a powerhouse of unrequited need and suppressed yearning. When it gets tapped, whoever is lucky enough to experience it with her had better hold on tight, because it's gonna be one hot as hell ride.

Me. I want it to be me.

Fuck. I shake off the notion and unload the mower.

I can't be that for her. I've got nothing in my well for the kind of loving Cher needs. She might be broken, but that just means she's got more pieces to love.

The vision of her plump lips and sad eyes haunts me as I begin to mow. By the time I'm done, I'm aggravated and unfit for company.

I'm champing at the bit to leave when my tormentor traipses outside looking as sweet and delicious in simple shorts and a t-shirt as the food in her hands. Her bare feet with pink toenails have me groaning and looking to the heavens for mercy.

You can't have her, I run on repeat, her curvy, petite frame keeping me captivated through the kitchen window as I wash my hands and splash cool water on my face.

Maybe I should pour some down my pants.

Deciding a wet spot in the front of my jeans would be more of a spectacle than the erection I'm fighting, I take a deep breath and face the fire.

Minutes tick by silently as I mindlessly devour the food on my plate instead of her. She's a study in self-control as she picks at her sandwich, her eyes barely landing on me more than a time or two since I sat down. But what I see in them has me fighting for air and courage. It's like she's begging me to be something—someone she needs.

Could I?

Could I love her? Could she love me? For now? Forever?

Christ, what it would be like to mow *our* lawn, eat lunch with her on the deck, then disappear inside to love her the way I'm convinced she's never known. Hell, I'm not sure I've known what it can truly be like between a man and a woman when they come together in love, lust, refuge from the cruelty of life. Could she be that for me? Could I be that for her?

She can barely look at me, though. I'm a broken fuck who can never give her what she needs. I'd break her. Irreparably.

I clear my throat and open up—or maybe close—the can of worms sitting between us.

"Gabriel is like a son to me."

Her brow rises in question. She knows this.

Fuck, I'm going to muck this up.

"I'll be your protector, Cher. Make sure no one ever hurts you again. Hell, I'll even be your friend, your confidant. If you need an ear to listen, I'm here." What is sure to be regret in my eyes locks on her confused gaze. "But I can't be your lover—"

Her surprise morphs into embarrassment as her skin pinkens, her head shaking.

Did I read her wrong?

"I never—"

I hold up a hand. "I know." I break eye contact, a reprieve from her weighted gaze, and search the yard, though I'm not really seeing it. "I don't even know if you want to be intimate with anyone, never mind me."

Fuuuuck! Why is doing the right thing so hard?

I find her wounded blue-eyed gaze as my next words scrape up my throat like they're barbed with glass, "I can't be that for you. I lost the ability to love and be loved a long time ago. I promised to never hurt you, and in order to keep that promise, I can't ever touch you."

The hurt and disappointment on her face guts me worse than her next words. "I never thought you would. I'm not..." She shakes her head, waving me off. "It's fine. Thanks for your honesty." She stands, collecting her plate and glass, leaving the pitcher of sweet tea and the rest of the food, and doesn't say another word as she steps in the house, locking the door behind her.

Not once, but three times.

Three deadbolts.

Each click of a lock cuts even deeper.

Honesty? If I was being honest, I would've told her being in her bed, in her life, in her heart would be next to heavenly. I haven't wanted a woman like I want her since Vera, and maybe not even then.

I sit for a few minutes more, not because I'm hoping she'll come back out, but because I'm mustering up the courage to walk away, leaving her thinking I don't want her. As terrible as it feels to admit my shortcomings to someone I want to think well of me, it'd be worse to let her think it's because there's something wrong with *her*.

It's a tragedy all on its own. Her dejected look, believing I could never want a woman like her. A woman with a past, demons who hurt her in ways I don't even know, yet read all over her face, and in the white scars I catch a glimpse of every now and then.

If she knew the truth, she'd run from me faster than if a pack of hungry wolves were chasing her.

The thing is, I *am* that hungry wolf.

And I'm fucking starving.

CHER

It's for the best. Really. I was being silly. Thinking a virile man like James could want a broken-down caboose like me, as many scars on the outside as in. No man wants that—needs what I have to offer. Besides, I could never be naked in front of a man again. Too much damage. I easily hide the worst of them behind my shirts. Germain loved my pain. He craved it as much as I feared it.

James is right. I don't want an intimate relationship. I don't need it.

I don't crave it. Except maybe the few times he's looked at me with na-ked yearning like I had something *he* needs—desires, maybe even craves.

But in a different way than I've experienced before.

I want to know what that *something* is. What could I possibly have that any other woman walking down the street couldn't give him?

I guess I'll never know.

He made sure to close that door.

I made sure to lock it from the inside.

There's no getting in.

There's no getting out either.

CHAPTER 7

CHER

PAST

THREE WEEKS PASS. NO SIGHT OR WORD FROM James. When a young man from a lawn mowing service shows up in James' place one day, I panic. I can't sit at home and watch a stranger mow my lawn, having him roaming around outside, so close—too close.

This is my sanctuary.

My safe place now that Germain no longer dwells between these walls. I may still be learning how to reclaim the space, but now a man I don't know is making a racket outside, like he's beating on the walls, trying to knock down the fortress around me...

Until this moment, I didn't realize how comforting the sound of the lawn mower was when I knew it was Cap at the helm. But a stranger? I can't...

And Cap knows me. He'd know... Unless... What if something happened to him?

My heart seizes with fear.

I grab Reese and set out for the gym. It's insane, but I have to know. I have to see for myself.

"Mom, where are we going?"

My frown and twisted lip are my only response as I focus on the road. Driving is not my favorite adulting duty. I didn't even learn how to drive until a few years ago. My father never taught me, and Germain would never think of allowing me such freedom. As a result, I'm a nervous driver—maybe nervous in general. I should pull over and let Reese drive, but this is something I need to do. A fear I need to conquer.

"Who was that guy mowing the lawn? Why didn't Cap come? Did you have a fight or something?"

My ever-intuitive girl hits the nail on the head. "I don't know." It's the truth, but not the entire truth. The last thing she needs to know is I'm attracted to a man I can never have, a man who could never want spoiled leftovers when he can dine on bone-in ribeye every night of the week.

As my nerves spike, I tell myself I'm only going to check on him, to see for myself that the man who's breathed new life into my son is okay. I'd never forgive myself if he wasn't.

Pulling around back, I'm thankful I don't have to try to find a parking spot on the street. Parallel parking is not my forte. It's not even in the realm of *I could get better if I practiced*. I barely passed the driving test. The only reason I did was I borrowed a Smart Car so tiny, even *I* could parallel park it. But a normal-size car, forget it. Never going to happen.

James' black truck is in the owner's parking spot. I pull in the reserved space next to it, knowing I won't be here long. I search Reese's frazzled face for signs of understanding or support. A lift of my brow has her shaking her head to my unspoken question.

She's not coming with me.

This is something I need to face alone. I leave the car running and wait after closing my door until she locks it, then wave my phone at her. She'll call if she needs anything.

Warren, James' operational manager, spots me before I can take three steps inside the gym and heads my way. He knows from past experience I have a bigger personal space bubble and not to get too close.

"Mrs. Stone? What brings you here?" His features morph into worry. "Is Gabriel alright?"

I hold up my hand. "He's fine." God, I hope he's fine. It's been a few weeks since he's called, but that's not unusual, depending on the mission. I clench my fists, nails biting into my palms. One battle at a time. I glance past Warren. "Is James here?"

He's seemingly relieved to hear I'm not here about Gabriel. "Cap is in his office. You good or do you want me to come with you?"

I step back. "No," and throw a "thank you" over my shoulder as I jog up the stairs and nearly trip over my myself on the third rung. Someone is going to kill themselves on these stairs someday. Apparently, it might be me. Stupid and clumsy.

The door to his office is partially closed, or partially open, depending on how you look at it. I see it as an invitation to come in without knocking. If he wanted—needed—privacy, he'd close his door.

I regret not knocking the second I push inside. I came to check on him, the man I've become accustomed to mowing my lawn, checking in on Reese and me in Gabriel's absence, who would never send a stranger to my home… Or so I thought.

Apparently, he had more important things to do.

Frozen, all I can think is *how did I not hear them from outside his door?*

James has a woman pinned against the wall, her skirt hiked up, her leg wrapped around his hip. She moans and grinds against him, pumping her hand up and down his cock between them as he kisses her stupid—or into an orgasm. Which, unfortunately for me—yay, for her—she does seconds later, begging him, "Fuck me, Cap. Fuck me hard."

CAP

Fuck, yes. She's so hot, and I haven't even been inside her yet.

I curl my index harder against her G-spot, and Jen falls apart beautifully for me, coming around my fingers as I kiss her harder, eating up her pleas, "Fuck me, Cap. Fuck me hard."

Her grip on my cock has me ready to blow before I can sink balls deep and fuck her against the wall. Not my favorite position but it's hot and quick. Just about the only way I like it nowadays—when I can't take it anymore and need the real deal my hand just can't compete with.

A gasp from behind has me groaning and turning toward the door.

Cher standing there with her hand over her mouth in total shock knocks the air out of my lungs.

"Cher." The ache in my chest is palpable. I pull away from my PA, not even concerned about her state of undress or mine.

My voice must pull Cher from her stupor as she shrieks and darts out the door.

"Fuck." I zip up my jeans and run after her, ignoring the whine from Jen. I never should have touched her. Especially at work—fuck, or anywhere. So fucking stupid.

"Cher, please."

"No." She darts around the corner, leaping for the stairs with surprising grace.

Her speed scares the shit out of me, though. I catch her around the waist just as her foot misses the first step. I haul her against me, ignoring her struggle, and growl in her ear as softly as I can muster so as not to scare her, "You could have fallen down those stairs. Shhh, Cher. Please give me minute to make things right."

She scoffs as if what I'm proposing is preposterous. Perhaps it is.

I'm not sure there's any coming back from what she walked in on. I'd be madder than Hades if I walked in on her nearly fucking another man.

I've no right, but my baser instincts don't give a fuck right now.

And I just want to make this right.

"Please," my plea does the trick. She stops fighting and lets me carry her into the nearest empty office, which happens to be Warren's. I close and lock the door—something I should have done earlier in my own damn office.

I should let her go, give her space, but I can't. "I want to hold you until you don't hate me." I practically curl around her, my arms banded around her front, her back to my chest, her feet barely skimming the floor, and my head buried in her neck. Her head is bowed, her breaths soft and stuttering. Is she crying or just trying to catch her breath?

"I'm sorry, Cher. I'm sorry you saw that."

"James."

"I'm sorry it happened at all." Christ, will she ever be able to look at me again? I know we have no future other than being friends, but until this very moment, I didn't realize how much the idea of losing our tenuous connection at all scares the hell out of me. "I'm so fucking sorry."

"Cap."

Fuck. She rarely calls me Cap. I'm always *James*. I'm so fucked. I've ruined everything.

"It's fine." She disentangles herself from me.

Even as I try to hold on, she so easily pushes my hands away—the hands that were all over another woman mere moments ago.

Inside another woman mere moments ago. I jam them inside my pockets, wanting to wash her off my skin.

The loss of holding Cher in my arms… I've never felt so crushingly empty.

She wipes at her eyes, though she won't look at me so I can confirm if it's tears or just messed-up makeup, or a self-soothing action as she composes herself.

"It's not fine." I step into her.

She steps back. "I only came to be sure you were okay. I was worried when some kid was mowing my lawn instead of you." She fidgets with hem of her shirt. "I let my worry get the better of me." Her gaze flits around the room. Shaking her head, she laughs without an iota of humor. "So stupid. I could have called." Her hands wave in the air in disgust. It seems more in contempt for herself than me.

That makes it hurt even more.

"You're always welcome here, Cher." As much as I hate to think it, yeah… If she'd only called first today…

A twist of lips and her sad blink stick the knife of regret further in my gut. Her soulful gaze locks on me. "I'm going to go."

I gently grab her wrist as she edges around me. "Please let me make this right."

"There's nothing wrong for you to make right." She doesn't look at me as she opens the door and slips out.

I don't follow. Though every instinct in me is yelling for me to do just that.

Don't let her go.

What can I say? What can I promise? What would I do differently? She and I aren't an item. I didn't cheat on her. I didn't hurt her, at least not physically.

There's nothing wrong for you to make right. Her words hurt more than her anger ever would—ever could.

I want there to be *something* between us, something *to break*, so I get to fix it. That would mean we were together—or *something*.

Nothing seems so much worse… emptier… more painful.

I didn't know that would be the last time I'd see her for over a year.

She pulled away. Shut me out.

The times when I did see her again, it was always fleeting. No *hello*. No welcoming smile to warm my heart, make me feel forgiven. It was a curt nod.

The day we welcomed Gabriel home from the Army for good, I was reminded of this fateful day that should have driven me far away from banging my assistants.

Turns out, it was the catalyst that set off a long string of bad choices and a revolving door of new assistant after new assistant. I'd be good for a few weeks—months, sometimes. But they'd give me that wanton look, ask if there was *anything else they could do for me?*

Not a single one of them had anything I needed, but it didn't stop me from trying to fill that hole in my chest where love used to live, where self-respect went beyond my business and into the man I was.

The man who vacated worthiness the day Vera married my half-brother.

Any remnants that remained were wiped clean the day I lost the possibility, any hope, of more with Cher. The day I pushed her so far into herself, she didn't leave her home for three years.

I did that.

I swore I'd never hurt her.

I broke what wasn't mine to break.

CHAPTER 8

CHER

PRESENT

IT'S NEARLY THREE IN THE MORNING WHEN I GET my first glimpse of my grandson, Maddox. He's big, just like his daddy. He has a head full of baby-soft hair, the color so dark black it's almost blue, just like his parents, Reese, and me. The nurse says his blue eyes may change, but I don't think so. They're just a shade or two lighter than the Stone family blues.

He's beautiful.

I fight the emotions that are quick to rise, never far from the surface, but so rarely shown. This is my son's day. The day he becomes a Daddy. The day he shines so bright my heart hurts. I should be beaming with joy. Instead, I'm full of regret, sorrow for past wrongs I can never hope to make right.

Leaning in, breathing in my grandson, I hide my wayward tears and whisper, "I swear I'll get it right with you, my sweet boy." Nothing, no one will hurt this boy if I have any say in the matter. Not that Gabriel or Frankie need my help. They've got it covered in ways I failed with my own children.

But still. I'm going to work my ass off to ensure my shut-in tendencies are behind me. I'm not agoraphobic, but you'd never know it by actions for more years than I care to admit. I want to be the protector to my grandson, not the other way around. Everyone feels they need to protect me when I'm the oldest here and supposed to be the wisest. I'll do everything I can to protect his innocence, be sure he has a childhood like his father never had.

I can never make it right with my kids, but I can*not* screw things up with theirs.

Gabriel pulls himself away from a sleeping Frankie to wrap me and his son in an encompassing hug. "Can you believe it, Mom? Me, a dad?"

He doesn't mean it. My son rarely has doubts. He has enough confidence to rule a kingdom and slay his demons. But sometimes… "I always knew you'd make a great husband and father. I saw it in you. The instincts were always there. You know Reese and I never would—"

"Don't," he cuts me off. "Don't bring *him* into this."

I nod. My son's right. I always say the wrong thing. "I just mean, you have a warrior's heart but a healer's soul. You were destined for this moment right here."

"Fuck, Mom."

I pat his chest and hand him his son, all bundled up and looking so small in his father's huge embrace. I kiss his cheek, then Reese's, with promises to see them tomorrow. I slip out before James returns with coffee for everyone.

He offered to take me home. I can't allow that. I've finally made it out of my house for more than groceries. Spending time with James might tip me into preservation mode. Again.

I let him down. Made him think I wanted more from him—that what he did wasn't enough—that he wasn't enough.

He's all I've thought about since I saw him in that animal state…

Seeing him again would bring the fantasies that have played in my head for the past four years to life. The sight of him making that woman come in his embrace. His passion, his focus, solely on her. Him devouring her in ways that felt good for her, not just for him.

Did she have any idea how lucky she is to know such passion? To experience it at all? To experience it with *him* specifically?

Stop. You don't want that. You can never *have* that.

I hurry around the corner and take the stairs. I can't chance running into James in the elevator.

Downstairs. just as I'm nearly free of the hospital, Jonah stops me. "Ms. Stone—"

"Cheryl," I remind him.

He smiles, embarrassed for the reminder. He's so very respectful, big and shy. I hope he finds the right woman to appreciate all that goodness inside him.

"I was popping up to see if they needed anything before heading home." He thumbs over his shoulder. "Do you need a ride?"

"No. Thank you, though. You go on and enjoy my grandson." I rush off before he can insist or see where I'm headed. None of these Black Ops men would ever let me walk to a taxi stand, much less let me take one. Gabriel will be pissed if he finds out.

An hour later, I'm finally home. Exhausted, I haul my butt to the shower. It's a habit I can't break—showering before bed. Germain always insisted—no matter what time it was.

Stripping, I neatly fold my clothes as I go, placing them on the bathroom counter to be placed in the laundry when I'm done.

I avoid my reflection. Somethings are better not seen. My nude form is one of those things. Reminders of Germain's rage tattoo my body. Forever marked by my children's father. The man who was supposed to be my savior turned destroyer.

Shivering, I rush through the cold shower. I save washing my hair until the morning. My brain turns on automatic, rerunning the day's events, logging them, determining which ones I deem successful and on which ones I fell short.

The reminder of my failure as a mother is the reason for the cold shower. My punishment. I don't deserve a warm, blissful escape. I deserve the biting-cold truth of reality.

CAP

I nearly trip over my own damn feet when I enter Frankie's hospital room to find Jonah holding Maddox and Cher nowhere in sight. I set the tray of coffees on the nightstand and hand one to Gabriel, when really, I want to dump them all in the trash and find the one person I might want to spend time with more than the new baby.

"She went home. If that's what you're all pissed off about." The humor in Gabriel's tone is enough to have my fists clenching in frustration and the need to hit something—someone. That knee-jerk reaction never eases. I've learned to tame it, but it's still there. I want to hit and fight as much as the men on my team.

Scrubbing the scruff on my jaw, I focus on Maddox sleeping soundly in Jonah's arms. "Why?"

"You know why, Cap." He kisses Frankie, who's still sleeping after the efforts of giving birth—and nods to Jonah. "You good?"

"Yeah, man." Jonah's gaze remains steady on Maddox.

With a hand on my shoulder, Gabriel directs me to the door. "Cap and I are gonna step in the hall. Call if either of them wakes up."

"Got it."

Outside Frankie's room, Gabriel leans against the wall, arms crossed, his eyes on the door.

I wait. He's got something to say. Something I'm sure I don't want to hear.

On a deep exhale, Gabriel finally says, "I owe you a lot, Cap. I'm partially the man I am because of you. I don't mean just my fighting career. Of course, that, but more. You taught me respect, control, and fighting for what you want both in and out of the ring."

A humble Gabriel is unexpected. "You don't—"

He stops me with a hand on my chest. "But," he presses forward till my back hits the opposite wall, "I don't know what happened between the two of you. She won't talk about it." His hand falls to his side.

I remain silent, unsure of where this is going, feeling I won't like it much.

"I'm not sure I want to know. I've let it slide all these years because I know how she is, and I know you." We lock eyes. "I trust you with my life, my family." His eyes well up.

I'm done for. "Son." I grasp his shoulder.

"You've been there for me, for my family when I couldn't be. But now I have a son. You"—he pokes me in the chest—"have a grandson. Whatever you have to do, make this right with Mom. If you have something to tell me, tell me. If you have something to ask me, ask me. But don't"—he pokes me hard enough to leave a bruise—"avoid it any longer." He steps back. "Make it right, Cap. Be the man you taught me to be. Be the man I *know* you are."

Fuck. Me.

He slips back into the room, leaving me knocked down and strung out. If I had any hand in making Gabriel who he is, I'm honored. I'm the humbled one by his admission, his strength in facing his fears and asking me to do the same.

He's right. I've avoided Cher for too long. And why?

Who has the space helped, really?

It's time to man up and make peace.

Fuck. This is going to hurt.

CHAPTER 9

CHER

AS I STEP OUT OF THE SHOWER, I'M STARTLED by banging on the front door and the incessant ringing of the doorbell. I take a deep breath to quell my rising panic and haphazardly dry off enough to jam my arms through the sleeves of my robe. With my phone poised to call 9-1-1 and my *be brave* mantra, I creep to the front door.

The relief that floods my system when I see it's James on the other side makes me light-headed. I don't think… I unlock the door and swing it open.

"Jesus, woman. What the fuck? I've been banging for five minutes." His chest is heaving as his gaze sweeps up and down my body. "I was ready to break down the door. I was worried something had happened to you."

He was worried about me? My skin breaks out in goosebumps from the heat of his gaze and the worry on his all too handsome face. James would make a mint as a model. The graying of his sideburns and stubble only adds to his alpha hotness. I swipe at the water dripping down my neck from the back of my still-wet hair. "I was in the shower."

He frowns. "Why are you shaking?" He steps through the door, gripping my shoulders. "Jesus, Cher. You're trembling from head to toe."

I'm locked in his arms, my head buried in his chest before I can answer.

"I did this. Shit, I scared you with the racket I made." He mutters a stream of cusswords, reaching back to shut and lock the door. "I'm sorry."

I can't say his intense arrival didn't scare me, but it's not why I'm shaking. "I'm cold from the shower." Why did I tell him that? He didn't need to know.

"Shower?" He sweeps me up in his arms and sits on the couch with me bundled on his lap, pulling the blanket I keep on the back of the couch over us. "Did your hot water heater go out?"

I shrug, not going *there* with him. The less he knows, the better. Besides, who can concentrate on words when he's got me all comfortable and bundled up in his arms? Have I ever felt this safe with a man?

"I'll look at it in the morning."

I glance at the clock on the mantel. "It is morning."

He chuckles. "Nearly. And neither of us has gotten any sleep." He holds me close, nuzzling my head under his chin. "I'm sorry, Cher." His heavy exhale and the thud of his heart have me sinking in further. "Sorry for all these years I let pass without making things right with you."

I freeze. "You didn't—"

"I know you said I didn't do anything wrong." He lifts my face to his. The sincerity of his gaze has my heart clamoring. "But I did. I was weak and took advantage of what was right in front of me, because I can't..." He shakes his head, eyes darting away, then back. "Anyway, I don't want to be at odds with you any longer. I want us to be friends. Do you think you can do that? Give me another chance, Cher?"

Friends? I'm not sure I'm up to being friends, but I'm pretty sure I'm not up for being anything else either. The years without him in my life have been hard—lonely. And he's not asking to be more than friends—which I doubt I'm capable of either.

His thumb brushes my cheek, the tender gesture making my eyes flutter closed.

"Forgive me, Cher." His warm breath caresses my skin as his lips press to my cheek. This feels like *more* than friendship.

Whatever this is, it feels right. "Okay."

"Okay?" His green eyes light up, and his rare dimpled smile appears.

I bite my lip to stop my smile from getting embarrassingly big.

"Damn." His gaze jumps to my lips and sticks. "You're still shaking."

I am, but it's for a whole other reason.

He leans in.

I hold my breath.

Closer.

Ohmygod. Is he? Could I?

I want him to.

I think…

"I wish…" he drifts off, blinks, clears his throat, and the moment is broken. He stands, setting me on the couch in his place, his hand scrubbing his scalp. "How 'bout I fix us some breakfast?"

Popping to my feet, I pull my robe tighter, feeling uncomfortably underdressed and a bit overwhelmed and sadly disappointed, which knocks me for a loop.

I can't have *more* with James. I can't have more with *anyone*.

Not just *can't*. I don't *want* more.

Do I?

It doesn't matter. He asked if I want to be *friends*. Obviously, I got swept up in all the body heat and blanket time.

"I, uh, I promised Gabriel I'd be back at the hospital this morning after I finish my baking. But I really need some sleep first."

For such a stoic man, his disappointment is palpable.

"Raincheck?" I offer as condolence. We just made up, after all. I can't avoid him—not forever anyway.

"Yeah, okay." He rounds the couch and stops at the door. "You want me to check your water heater before I go?"

God, no. "I got it." *I so don't.* Thankfully, there's nothing wrong with my water heater. Gabriel had it replaced last month. It works like a dream.

"Maybe I'll see ya at the hospital later."

"Yep. Maybe." Probably not.

He opens the door and turns. "Cher?"

"Hmm?"

"I'm serious. I'm not going to let you avoid me. We're friends. Friends hang out—see each other."

Do friends sit on each other's laps? Caress and kiss their cheek?

Do friends make you weak in the knees, ache in your heart, and regret your broken past?

If that's a *yes*, then I guess we're friends.

If not, then I'm royally screwed, 'cause I really liked being on his lap.

"I can see that." I move to close the door. "See ya, friend."

His crooked smile has my stomach flipping. "See ya, Cher."

CAP

I should go home and get some sleep, but I'm too amped up. Instead, I hit the gym, shower, drink a million cups of coffee, drink a protein smoothie, get a little work in, then head back to the hospital to bring Frankie the Chinese food she's been craving. It's close to lunchtime, but it wouldn't matter. I'd do anything to bring her the food she wanted, even if I had to beat down the door to wake up the owner of our favorite place. Luckily, he's a friend and more than happy to pull together enough takeout to feed an army—or Frankie and Gabriel's massive appetites.

"Oh, my god, Cap. Tell me that's what I think it is." Frankie jumps out of bed pretty darn fast for a woman who gave birth less than twelve hours ago, accosting the bags in my hands.

I hand them over. "Yeah, honey. All your favorites…" Gabriel saunters out of the bathroom, drying his hair with a towel. "And even the big guy's favorites too."

"The pancake things?" His eyes light up.

"Yes, the pancake things or better known as moo shu pork."

He snaps his fingers, "That's the one," then kisses Frankie on the cheek before digging into the bags.

"Where's my grandson?" I stare at the empty spot his bassinet was in last night—or more likely, early this morning.

Frankie's head pops up; surprise morphs into acceptance in her glistening gray eyes. My girl—my daughter by choice—has no idea how much I love her. What I'd do to see her happy and safe. How proud I am of the woman, wife, and now mother she's become.

"Bath and routine tests," Frankie mumbles around the eggroll she's trying to devour in one bite.

Maybe I should have brought more.

"Sit, Cap. Eat." With a steely grip on my shoulder, my son-in-law urges me into a seat next to his bride at the small table in their room. It's not like I was planning on leaving without seeing Maddox.

I dish up some food for myself, roll a moo shu pancake for Frankie and set it on her plate. "How you feeling?"

"Hmm," she shrugs, "Sore, but pretty good, I guess. I've nothing to compare it to."

Gabriel stops mid-chew; his eyes flash with heat staring across the table. "She's fucking Wonder Woman, Cap. Never been so awed or proud."

"Big Man." Frankie sniffs.

Gabriel leans up and kisses her brow. "Eat, Angel. Our boy will be starving when he gets back." His eyes meet mine. "Maddox is breastfeeding like a champ."

"Of course he is. He'll be an ox like his father."

"That's it." Gabriel's fist lands hard on the table.

Frankie jumps. "Shit! What's it?"

Gabriel smiles. "Maddox's nickname. Ox. It's perfect."

"I kinda like Madman," Frankie pouts.

"Trust me. You don't want a madman for a son. You want an ox, Angel. Madman gets in trouble. Gets in fights because he'll have to prove his madman status. Ox doesn't start fights; he finishes them."

"Just like his daddy." She beams at him.

Damn, these two. They make it seem easy when I know it's anything but. "I'm proud of you two. Fighting through your issues to find the other side." I meet both their gazes. "Damn proud."

Gabriel nods, taking a beat before asking, "Did you take care of that issue?"

His mom. "I'm working on it."

"Good."

"What issue?" Frankie asks as she digs into the lo mein.

"Man stuff, Angel."

"What, like farts and cars?"

Gabriel laughs. "Yeah, just like that."

She doesn't prod, too busy eating. Thankfully. I'm not ready to discuss what's going on with Cher.

Fuck, I'm not even sure, myself. I've missed her these past years, and I still feel the pull as though we never spent a day apart.

Years. How the fuck did I let that happen? I've never been one to avoid conflict, but fuck, the idea of hurting her further makes me lose my appetite. The idea of never having *anything* with her is worse.

I was damn near ready to kiss her, right there in my lap, feeling all kinds of *mine.* Shocking the hell out of me.

You've thought of kissing her before.

Yeah, but she's never been near naked, trembling from I'm not sure what, and looking ready and willing to be devoured.

Devoured. By *me.*

It's not like I'm not attracted to her. I've always seen the beauty in Cher. She's a knockout. Natural and unassuming, with undeniable curves and suppressed or unrealized sexuality. She hits all of my buttons and a few I didn't even know I had.

Friendship. That's what I offered her. That's what she agreed to.

I can do friendship.

It's safe. Uncomplicated.

Doable.

Nice. But I want to be more than *nice* to Cher. I want to be *sweet.* I want to be *something.*

I hang around long enough to see Ox, dote on Frankie, and reassure Gabriel he's got it all in the bag.

Heading to the gym, I've got a million things to follow up on, but only one thing—one woman—on my mind.

Damn, doesn't seem like *friendship* at all.

CHAPTER 10

CHER

THE NEXT MORNING, DESPITE MY RESTLESS sleep, I'm up earlier than normal. The first batch of goodies is out of the oven, and I'm just about to put in the second batch when there's a soft rap at the door.

My mind flashes to James and him beating down my door last night. Flushed at the thought of those near-kisses, I startle when I see his face staring back at me through the peephole.

"Morning, Cher." His head tilts like he knows I'm watching him. "Open up, Sugarplum. Let me in." He holds up his hands. "I brought breakfast."

I unlock and open the door. "Sugarplum?" I'm not sure if I love or hate the term of endearment.

He chuckles. "It got you to open the door." He slips past me, not allowing me a second to protest. "I know you're busy, but you need to eat too." He glances over his shoulder on his way to the kitchen. "Come on. Food's not getting any hotter."

Shaking my head, I ignore the growl in my stomach, close and lock the door. "Are you gonna always be such a nuisance, coming over at all hours of day or night?"

"Is that an invitation, Sugarplum?"

I quirk a brow. Yeah, still not sure. Sugarplum.

"Plum? You know," he sets down the coffee carrier and the bag of what I assume is food on the kitchen table, "I'm a damn good spooner." He flashes me a wicked smile. "I'd even let you be the big spoon."

What the? "Big spoon?"

He stands back, cupping his hands, palm to back. "You know... big spoon to little spoon. Spooning." His smile turns incredulous. "You're kidding, right? You do know what spooning is?"

I shrug and grab plates from the cabinet and napkins from the counter. Of course I've seen cuddling on TV. I've just never heard the *big spoon* referenced or experienced anything as tender as *spooning*.

"You're serious." He swipes his face with his palm. I've shocked him.

If he only knew how many things I know so little about, he'd be in shock all day. I motion to the table. "What's for breakfast?"

His eyes search mine for a moment longer, then he nods, silently agreeing to move on. "Omelets, hash browns, and pancakes."

"Sounds delicious, thank you."

With a quick squeeze of my shoulder, concern still shines in his eyes. "My pleasure."

"Let me just get this batch in the oven." I turn away, unable to take the pity I'm sure will replace concern at any moment. My social avoidance skills are well earned and all too easy to fall back on.

When you never know how your husband will respond at any given moment or situation, you become an expert at dodging and avoiding, becoming small and invisible. When you have marks, scars all over your body, you learn to stay at a distance. Things always seem so much... nicer, at a distance. Up close is where the dirtiness lives, where the devil dwells, and where shame resides.

Up close I can't hide, can't unsee, can't pretend I don't wear my shame like armor all over my skin.

Timer set, I join James at the table. But before I can sit, he pulls the chair out for me.

In a blink of an eye, my breath stops, my hands shake, and the chair goes blurry as I continue to stare at his innocuous gesture.

He pulled the chair out for me.

Germain used to do that before he'd…

This isn't Germain. This is James.

He doesn't… He wouldn't.

"Cher?" James grips my arm. "You're as white as a ghost. What's wrong?" His hold tightens. "Fuck. Breathe! Cher, take a fucking breath."

I steal air into my lungs and press the back of my hand to my mouth, fighting back bile and tears, both threatening to explode out of my face at an embarrassing speed.

I turn away.

This is Cap.

He didn't mean it the same way Germain did. He wouldn't.

Warmth blankets my back; strong arms wrap around me, pulling me off my feet and onto his lap, probably sitting on the stupid chair he so kindly pulled out for me. "God, Cher, tell me what I did that set you off?"

I shake my head and bury my face in his chest.

Stupid, stupid, stupid. You're a stupid cunt. I flinch from the sound of Germain's voice, echoing from my memories.

"Shhh, baby. I got you. It's alright. Whatever spooked you is not really happening. I promise, whatever's in your head, I'd never do. Never, Cher. You understand me?"

I nod, struggling to separate my embarrassment and fear from the reality he's presenting. I know what I thought is not really happening. But muscle memory is strong, and mine was screaming, *don't sit down; it's a trick.*

He's gotta think I'm crazy. "Are you ready to rescind your friendship yet?" I all but blubber into his shirt.

"No, Cher. Never." He rubs soothing circles on my back, slowly rocking. I'm nearly asleep when his hand brackets the back of my neck and softly squeezes as he whispers, "Tell me what he did, Plum. Tell me, and let me carry it for you."

Carry it for me? I pull back, wiping my face with my sleeves, and he stops me, cupping my face in his big hands, swiping at my tears with his thumbs. His eyes are so gentle, full of remorse and understanding.

"Tell me. Unsaddle it and drop it at my feet. He's not here. He'll never hurt you again. I swear to you." He doesn't remove his hands; he keeps me there, locked in his determined gaze.

When I bite my lip to quell more tears, he releases it with his thumb. "That beautiful lip never did anything to you, Plum. Stop punishing it."

I smile at his insistence to call me *Plum*. Surprisingly, it's growing on me. I've never had a nickname before, unless you call *Stupid Bitch* or *Useless Whore* nicknames.

"Germain was many things, but a gentleman was not one of them."

James nods, his hands dropping to my hips, squeezing softly, encouraging me to continue.

"When he was feeling particularly cantankerous, he'd pull my chair out for me. Wait for me to sit and pull it out at the last second so it'd be too late to catch myself. I had a bruised tailbone more times than not." So stupid. Saying it out loud, Germain was so childish, petty, besides just plain mean.

James grip tightens, his jaw clenching.

"He'd laugh that I'd fall for it every time. I didn't, of course. But if I didn't sit, he'd beat me right there in front of the kids for not trusting him. He'd usually beat me anyway, but it was always worse if I'd been disobedient beforehand." My gaze drops to my lap.

He cups my cheek. "And when I pulled out the chair for you, you thought—"

"I didn't." I grab his wrist. "Not really." I tap my head. "Sometimes it gets mixed up in here. Memory or reality. The fear from the trauma is so palpable, it's hard to ignore sometimes, no matter how hard I try or want to. It's—"

"Still there."

"Yeah."

He pulls me in, cupping my face to his shoulder. "I'll kill him, Plum. I swear, if he ever comes near you again, or if I see him out somewhere, I'll gut him where he stands."

I don't doubt a word he says. James is a Black Ops Marine. The best of the best. Nobody messes with him or what or *who* he deems as *his*.

Does that mean he considers me *his?* "Cap."

"Shhh, Cher." He motions to the table. "Let me warm up this food and feed you. By the smell of it, the sweets in the oven will be done soon."

I smile, glancing at the timer on the microwave. "You've got a good nose. I can always tell when something is ready before the timer goes off too."

He kisses my cheek, then locks gazes with me. "Thank you for letting me in. I won't take advantage of your trust or let you down. Promise. I got you."

"Who's got you, Cap?"

His smile is heartbreakingly sexy at my use of his nickname of sorts. "You do, Cher. You do."

Damn, I do. And if I didn't, I would now that he'd gifted me with that honor.

CAP

My morning is shot, but for a good reason. Cher needed me. I don't know if she's ever shared the details of her history with her ex. Gabriel and Reese know because they were there, not because she confided in them.

I'm honored. Though I did insert myself into her nightmare, I couldn't let her slink away and hide when I triggered her awful memory.

Germain. Such an asshole. "A dead asshole."

"What?" Web answers.

Shit. Talking out loud about murder. Stealthy. "Nothing."

"No, I heard you. Who's a dead asshole? Need help?"

"I do, actually."

"And here I thought this was a social call."

"Not today, man. Sorry."

"No worries. Tell me about this asshole. What can I do?"

I debate for a moment if I want him hurt, warned, or found. "Find him."

"Done," Web confirms.

I rattle off the details I know about Germain Stone. If he's out there, Web will find him. And when he does… Well, let's just say, Germain Stone will know the wrath of Captain Jimmy Durant and the consequences of hurting his family—*my* family now.

CHAPTER 11

CHER

AS THE WEEKS GO BY, MY GRANDSON GROWS AT exponential rates. His giggles are music to my ears and a healing salve to my heart. I promised I'd get out more to help Frankie and become a familiar face to Maddox. I take them dinner a couple times a week, do a little light cleaning, kiss Ox's chubby cheeks, and skedaddle. It's an important time for them to bond as a family. They don't need me in the way. Maybe I'll help out more when Gabriel goes back to the gym full-time. Though, I have a feeling it won't be until Frankie is ready to go back to work. *If* she goes back.

I need to talk to James about building on a flex space that can be used as a nursery or someday, a daycare. Gabriel is the first, but he won't be the last to have babies. Maybe making the elite gym more family-friendly, his fighters can train more often and concentrate knowing their little bundles are safe and close.

Gabriel is struggling. He doesn't want to miss out on fights or let the guys, the gym, or James down. But he also wants to be there for Frankie and his son. He's nothing like his father. Thank the heavens. Gabriel wants to be present and accounted for in the lives of his family. He showed me that trait early on. He's always been a protector, a healer. Maybe if he and Frankie can bring Ox to the gym, they'll both feel better about pursuing their dreams—their careers—without feeling like they're missing out or letting someone down.

I rush through the cleanup, my baking done for the day. Tom should be here shortly to pick up today's order. I'd love to get some more clients, but I'm honestly not sure I can produce more in my small, noncommercial kitchen. Gabriel put in a double oven a few years back. It's helped. I'd never be able to meet Tom's growing demands without it, or without baking all night to have the goods fresh and ready by his late morning pick-up time.

As I box up the cakes, pies, and tarts, my mind wanders to James. He's been coming for breakfast nearly every day for the past few weeks. But today he had a breakfast meeting with a promoter. Reese worked hard on the presentation for the meeting. I pray it's going smoothly. I think the meeting relates to Rowdy's big fight. I'm not sure. I'm not the best at listening when they start talking shop. My mind usually wanders to the next day's orders and what I need to do to prep or buy.

Someday, I'll have my own bakery, if I'm lucky.

Don't be silly, Cheryl. No one would come to buy your desserts.

"Get out of my head," I whisper into the empty kitchen.

It's an old argument. Germain never believed in my dreams. He was happy enough to eat my food, my sweet treats, and punish me if there wasn't anything "interesting" around to eat. But the minute my dreams involved me leaving the house… Well, he wasn't having it. I rub at the last scar he gave me for suggesting it. It's behind my left ear, jagged and rough from lack of stiches. I'm lucky it didn't get infected.

When I hear Tom's van pull up the driveway, I wash and dry my hands, quickly inspect today's order, and open the door before he knocks.

"Good morning, Cheryl."

"Morning, Tom." I step back to let him pass. I'm not sure when he stopped calling me Mrs. Stone. Probably somewhere around the time he took over running the business for his father. It doesn't really bother me, but sometimes the way he says it does.

Like today, it's a little too sweet, a little too peppy. He eyes roam my legs before coming back up. I might be short and in my early forties, but even I know I have nice legs. His appraisal has me wishing I'd put on jeans. My cutoff shorts seem entirely too short, and my simple tank a little too revealing.

I am decent, and besides that, I shouldn't have to worry about covering up in my own home. Germain also dictated what I wore. Never again.

I slip by Tom. "Everything's ready."

"Good." He follows close behind. I swear I can feel his eyes on my rear.

"You always smell so good." He stands too close when I stop in front of the boxes.

I brush off his compliment with a wisp of a smile and a fake laugh. "Side effect of the job."

He props himself against the kitchen table, arms crossed, gaze directed at me, no intention of taking a load of boxes yet. "I hear you're seeing Jimmy Durant." His tone is accusatory and a tad hostile.

If he thinks my social life is any of his business, he's got another thing coming. "Not that it's any of your business, but I'm not seeing anyone." I collect a stack of boxes and shove them into his chest. He either has to catch them or ruin a large portion of his desserts. I step back. "Let me get the door for you."

His eyes... For a moment I fear he's not going to follow, but I turn and take a sound breath when I hear his steps behind me. I leave the door open when he exits and head back for another load. Maybe I should have done this all along, not allowing him in the house, but handing the boxes over at the front door. I've got containers ready for him when he returns.

He glares and swiftly relieves me of my load. "You don't have to do this. I don't mind getting them from the kitchen."

I shake my head. "I don't mind." I turn to collect the last batch, leaving him to watch or load up his van.

The last of the boxes handed off, I close the door, hoping he'll get the message and leave. Regrettably, I realize I haven't been paid. *Shoot.*

When I open the door, he's standing there with a smug smile and a raised brow. "Looking for this?" He flips up the envelope in his hand.

I nod and reach for it, but he's too quick.

He snatches it, tucking it into his back pocket. "I think it's time we address this thing between us."

My eyes must be bulging out of my head because my shock is pulsing in my ears. "I'm sorry?"

He pushes forward, forcing me to step back. "We've known each other for what? Ten years now?" He closes the door behind him. "You were hot as fuck back then, but now?" He bites his lip. "Damn, you age better than a fine wine."

Panic has me backing up, needing to put distance between us, but in my haste, I trip over my own heel. He catches my arm, stopping my backwards tumble, but now I'm pressed to his chest, his arm banded around my back.

"See? Like in one of those romance novels I've seen you reading. I caught you before you fell."

I struggle, trying to yell, but fear has taken my ability to speak. I sound like a dying cat.

"I've been patient." He fingers the neckline of my tank top. "Downright saintly, if you ask me."

"T-Tom." I push against his chest. "Stop."

"Stop? You'll give that old man a piece, but not me?"

My palm connects with his cheek with a *thwap.* My hand stings, but I ignore the discomfort and manage to wiggle out of his grasp.

I pull my phone from my pocket and speed dial the only person I think can help me as I continue to back up into the kitchen.

"Tom. Stop this. There's nothing between us." I round the kitchen island. "There never was." I glance at my screen and see the call connected and call duration counting up. "There never will be."

His laugh is menacing. Lightning fast, his slap across my face takes me to my knees, my phone skittering across the floor. He grips my face between his thumb and fingers, squeezing.

I cry out, latching onto his wrist, trying to pry him off.

"You think *he* can give you something I can't? You think he really wants you? You're just a fast fuck. He's a player. Everyone knows that."

He releases me with a shove, and my head connects with the cabinet. "He can have your frigid used-up cunt. I'm done waiting on you to see me."

The room spins. I can't…

His shoes slip out of sight as I fall to the side, barely catching myself before my head hits the floor. I blink a few times, fighting unconsciousness.

I win, barely.

CHAPTER 12

CAP

I WAS ALREADY ON MY WAY OVER TO SURPRISE CHER with lunch. I've never been so thankful in my life to only be a block from her house. I don't know what I thought I'd hear when I answered her call, but it certainly wasn't her shaky voice, telling Tom *stop* and that there was *nothing between them, never would be*, or the nasty things he said back to her.

I want to rip his face off through the phone. Then beat the shit out of him. I never cared for the guy or the way he looked at her.

White-knuckling the steering wheel, I floor it. *Hold on, Plum. I'm coming.* And I'm going to murder Tom if he's stupid enough to still be there.

God, what happened? Is Tom the kind of guy to get physical?

Fuck.

Pulling into her driveway, I barely get the car in park before I'm barreling toward the front door. I nearly knock it off its hinges when I swing it open. It being unlocked is the first warning that she is not okay.

"Cher!"

No answer. More warning bells go off.

"Cher!" I bellow as I rush to the kitchen. Her groan reaches me seconds before I see her lying on the floor, her eyes closed.

"Jesus Christ, Cher." I fall to my knees next to her and check her pulse, though I can see she's breathing from the rise and fall of her chest. I'm relieved to find her pulse is steady and strong. "Cher, honey, can you hear me? Open your eyes."

"James," she mumbles and groans as she blinks.

I hover over her, fighting to remain calm as she tries to focus on me. "There you are."

"T-Tom," she stutters.

"He's gone."

She nods but winces and groans.

"Did he do this? Did you hit your head?"

"Mmm, yes."

I want to pick her up. But, fuck, I don't know how badly she's hurt. I could make it worse if her neck's hurt too. "I should call the police."

Her eyes fly open. She grips my arm. "No. No police. No Gabriel or Reese. Promise."

"Cher." I disagree.

"Promise, Cap."

"Fuck." I glance around for one of her kitchen towels.

"Promise"—she tries to sit up—"or leave."

"Fuck, you're stubborn, Plum."

She glares at me.

"Fine. Fuck! I promise."

She manages to sit up with my help, and I finally notice the area around her. The back of her head, her shirt, the floor are covered in blood. Jesus.

"Cher, I promised not to call the police or your kids, but I'm taking you to the hospital. You could have a concussion or need stiches." I expect her to argue.

She simply blinks and gives a single nod. Her acquiesce is concerning. I know Cher doesn't care much for doctors or hospitals.

"I'm going to pick you up. Okay?"

"Hmm."

I set her on the island so I can inspect her head. She's got a gash a few inches long. "You're definitely gonna need stitches." I press my forehead to hers, taking a second to catch my breath. She's okay. She'll be fine. "You scared the shit out of me, Plum."

CHER

Turns out the cut on my head wasn't as bad as James made it out to be. Instead of stiches, I have a few staples and orders to not wash my hair for twenty-four hours. I'm not happy about having to live with dried blood in my hair. The good news, I have a mild concussion, and my hair covers the damage, so no one other than James needs to know what happened.

I refused to file a police report. I'm not pressing charges. I just want to forget the incident ever happened. I need to focus on moving forward. Figure out how I'm going to make a living, given I won't be working with Tom any longer.

"I'm fine to go home," I think I say for the tenth time since we left the emergency room, heading for his house.

"And what if Tom comes back?" he finally replies, upset I won't press charges, get Tom locked up where he belongs.

I shiver at the thought. "Okay." I doubt the outcome of pressing charges would be Tom locked up. Maybe a fine, more than likely a slap on the wrist and a wink on his way out of the police station. I've been there. It's a good ole boy's club. Roughing up a woman, your kids, is no cause for alarm in my experience with the Vegas police. I'm sure some officers care. I've just never found one who did.

Given I wasn't bleeding to death, James grabbed a few things for me and threw them in an overnight bag. I've no idea what he managed to get in the few seconds he was willing to leave me, holding the kitchen towel to my head. He never planned on me returning home today.

"Besides, we have the BBQ tomorrow. You were going to come over early to help anyway. Now, you'll already be there."

He makes spending the night with him sound so convenient and practical, when I know it's about him keeping me safe and close. I've never seen the man so worried, his composure shattered as I blinked up at him from the kitchen floor. I was flooded with relief, knowing I'd be okay— safe—now that he was there.

"Thank you." My head rolls to the side to stare at him as he drives.

He squeezes my hand, his anger waning. "No thanks needed." He squeezes again, longer this time. "I'm just thankful you're alright."

Me too. It could have been much worse. What is it about me that screams *abuse me*?

"Hey." He shakes my hand. "Wake up. No sleeping. Not for a few more hours. We'll get some food in you, maybe a hot bath, then you can sleep."

I blink out the window. I didn't even realize I was falling asleep. I adjust, sitting up straighter and focus on staying awake.

Did I lead Tom on? Did I give him the wrong impression?

Tease, Germain invades my thoughts.

I need a cold shower.

I've heard talk of his home, but the wrap-around porch has me dreaming of swings and lazy mornings drinking coffee overlooking the lake. I'm lost in thought long after the sight is gone and he's pulled into the garage. I startle when he opens my door. He only smiles with a slight display of a dimple, unbuckles my seatbelt and lifts me into his arms.

"I can walk," I remind him.

He kisses my temple. "I know."

He's been doing that a lot since we've agreed to be *friends*. I'm still not convinced it's a friend type of gesture. Yet I don't mind. I've never been kissed on my temple, my forehead or my cheek, or anywhere else that was gentle and not demanding and only a prelude to hard, *I don't care if you enjoy it* kisses.

Germain rarely kissed me, except when we first started dating. The aggressive pre-wedding kisses transformed into demanding, almost always make me bleed post-wedding kisses. The more I hurt, the more he enjoyed it.

"Hey." James' gentle swipe of my cheek draws my eyes to him kneeling before me as I sit on a bed.

When did he get there?

When did I get here?

He swipes again, both cheeks this time, and rising up, he pulls me into his chest. "Don't cry, Cher. You're safe here. You're safe with me."

The tears I didn't know were falling only increase with his tender declarations. "Don't be nice to me, Cap. You'll only make it worse."

He chuckles. "I'm not afraid of a few tears, Plum." He pulls me down to him, my legs straddling his massive thighs, his arms holding me like a security blanket. "I'm not afraid of anything you give me."

I melt into him, relishing the strength of his sculpted body that manages to hold me so tight yet tenderly. James is a gentle beast of a man. His stoic silence is one I can relate to, but this possessive nurturer is taking me by surprise.

Why isn't he married or have kids of his own? He'd be great at both. That's obvious.

"Dammit, Cher."

I scowl at his looming face. "What—"

"You fell asleep again." He trails his worried gaze over my face as he examines me.

"Stop being so darn comfortable then."

He laughs. "Cute and funny." He stands, setting me on my feet as he does. "Come on. Let me feed you."

In his massive kitchen he proceeds to make bacon and eggs. The smell is intoxicating. "I've always loved the smell of bacon."

He brings over a slice on a paper towel to me sitting on an island stool where he ordered me to *stay*. "There's lots more. I'm a bit of a bacon fiend."

"I can see that." He has to be frying up a whole package just for the two of us.

"I bake mine in the oven. It's less work and mess." Ohmygod! My hand flies to my mouth. I spoke out of turn and criticized him. I hold my breath, waiting.

He frowns, studying me for a moment before shrugging and returning his focus to the stove. "You'll have to show me next time."

That's it? No reprimand for mouthing off, thinking I know better than him?

No more talking, Cher. Keep your hands on your lap and eyes downcast.

Be little. Be invisible. Don't make waves.

Be little. Be invisible.

Be little.

CHAPTER 13

CAP

THE FEAR ON HER FACE AFTER SHARING HER expertise on cooking bacon guts me. I brushed it off as if I didn't notice. But, fuck, she's practically shaking in her seat.

I will kill that motherfucker if I get the chance. No doubt in my mind. He's caused entirely too much damage to this gentle woman sitting in my kitchen hoping I don't notice her. Hoping I'll forget she exists. *I see you, Cher. I won't let you hide from me.*

Not to mention the pain and suffering her ex caused to Gabriel and Reese.

The first time Reese had a meltdown at the gym, I had to leave the building before I ripped someone's head off. I haven't been that angry, had the need to kill or be killed since… Vera.

Damn, I haven't thought about her in a long time. I bundled up those memories, that hurt and anger, and buried it a long time ago. *Go away,*

Vera. I don't need the anguish you bring. I've got enough regret going on in this kitchen. I don't need to add you to it.

Silence is all that greets me as I finish cooking.

Setting a plate piled with more food than I know she can eat in front of her at the island bar, I tip her chin, ignoring the fear still languishing in her blue-as-the-ocean eyes. "You don't sequester yourself in my house. You don't edit your thoughts or feelings. You're safe here." I wipe at the tears that silently streak down her cheeks. "You're safe with me, Cher."

"James." The pain infused in my name rips at the barbed wire around my heart.

My forehead meets hers. "I got you."

The scary thing is, I think she's got me too.

It's hours later. A catnap for her with me watching over her to be sure she's not suffering from any concussive side effects, more food, and seeing her to bed. I walk the hall until I know she's deep in sleep. Then I shoot off a text.

Fifteen minutes later I'm ushering Jonah into the kitchen, handing him a bottled water. "I'll be gone like an hour. Tops."

He eyes me speculatively. "Anything I should know?"

My gaze drifts past him to the stairs. "She's sleeping. I doubt she'll wake up, but if she does, let her know you're here—hopefully before she sees you. And for God's sake, don't scare her."

He chuckles. "I don't usually scare women, Cap. That's you and Gabriel's cuppa."

"I don't scare women." I scowl, slipping my phone into my pocket, and palm his keys.

"You keep telling yourself that." He finds this whole situation entirely too funny.

"Call if—"

"I got it." He stands straighter like he's getting ready to salute me. "Nothing comes between me and her."

I slip out quietly, taking Jonah's car. I don't want to chance waking Cher when the garage opens. I even considered rolling the car down the drive to ensure the engine starting doesn't do it, but he parked on the street like I'd asked.

She's a light sleeper, ready to jump at the slightest sound. I discovered that while she napped. I swear she woke just because I combed my hand through my hair. She'd have made a good lookout in the Marines. Always on guard. Ready. The reason though… fuels the fire in my gut, the clench of my fist, and the determination in the success of my mission.

I arrive just as they're closing, slipping silently through the unlocked back door, sticking to the shadows. You never realize how many dark corners there are until you live and die by them. Passing the kitchen, I take an assessing glance at the servers cleaning up the dining room, then continue to the back, beyond the storage room to the office.

I'm met with silence until I hear a moan, then another. I was listening to be sure he was alone, but whether he is or not, whatever is happening on the other side of that door can only make my task that much easier. Phone at the ready, I test the knob and *tsk* to find it unlocked. Fucking idiot made this too easy.

Opening it slowly, they don't notice until it's too late. I've already got them on video. Her head pulled back by his grip on her hair and him riding her from behind like he's drilling for gold. She's beautiful, but I doubt there's gold in that pussy. I don't say a word, I just keep recording, eating it up when he slaps her ass, and she cries out, saying his name, "Tom, please, Daddy!" in that sultry voice of hers.

I knew I didn't like the guy. I just couldn't put my finger on why. I'm becoming more and more aware as the seconds tick by. He's a skeezy, cheating, abusive motherfucker, not to mention incestuous. The woman he's banging is not only the local DA's wife, she's also his sister.

I think I might be sick.

I've seen enough. I close and lock the door, keeping the video running as their heads swivel to me, mouth and eyes wide as saucers.

I stop them before they can say a word. "I'm not here for you, Carolina, but I suggest you dress and scurry on home. Daniel wouldn't be too pleased to know the compromising position I found you in. I imagine he'd revert to his training if he knew *who* you were fucking."

Daniel and I go way back. We were in the Marines together. That blood runs deep. Deeper than her cheating, brother-fucking ass.

"Oh, Jesus. You wouldn't, Cap. Please," she whimpers.

"Like I said. I'm not here for you. But your fate lies in Tom's hands. Did he tell you he assaulted a woman today? Do you get off on that kind of foreplay?" I accuse, watching him but wondering if she does too.

She pushes off the desk and rounds on Tom, adjusting her dress. "What did you do?"

Tom casually tucks his flaccid dick back into his slacks. Maybe that was why he was going at her so hard—he couldn't *get hard*. "It was nothing—no one." He glares at me.

I look at my phone, act like I'm getting ready to make a call. "I think I'll let Gabriel 'No Mercy' Stone know you think his mother is a no one."

"Oh my God! You didn't," she screeches.

Tom pales, stammering, "I… She's a tease."

I rip him off his feet by the grip on his neck and slam him against the door. "Say that again."

"I-I didn't mean it. I've always liked her."

"Don't I know it." His sister pouts, taking a seat in his office chair. "He used to make me beg to suck his cock, calling me Mrs. Stone. Telling me how my—her—chocolate cake made him hard."

Jesus. These two.

"Shut it, Caro," Tom squeaks as my grip tightens.

"Here's the thing," I tighten my grip, watching his face redden, "you touched my family. You hurt what's *mine*. You took away Cheryl's livelihood. You're going to compensate her monetarily to my satisfaction, or I'll visit my good friend Daniel and show him the depth of your sisterly love. I may even let it slip to the press. Imagine how fast your successful restaurant business will go up in flames. You'll both be ruined."

Carolina jumps to her feet. "You wouldn't do that. You'd hurt Daniel too."

True. "Then let's be sure this gets resolved now." I release him and step back, giving him room to breathe and slip to the floor.

"Give him what he wants," she begs her brother. "Whatever it is."

He nods at her.

"How much?" she asks me. I guess I know who really has the balls in their twisted relationship.

"How much does lost income, a bruised face, stapled scalp, and silence go for these days?" I question like I don't have a clue. I've got a figure in my head, but I'm dying to see how much they'll throw at the problem to make it disappear.

Before I can speak, I hold up my hand. "And before you think you can double-cross me, remember who my family is. I've got military-trained special forces soldiers in my gym and at my fingertips, not to mention contacts at all levels of the government, as well as some in not nearly as savory places. You can run, but you can't hide from me. You can't throw anything at me that I can't come back at you with ten times over. So, think carefully before you speak, plot, or insult me with a measly number."

CHAPTER 14

CHER

I STIR AS THE BED SHIFTS AND STRONG ARMS WRAP around me from behind. "Shhh, Plum. I just need to hold you, be sure you're alright. Is that okay?"

"Yes," I answer too fast. I'm better now, knowing he's here.

I woke a bit ago and found Jonah asleep on the couch. Rather than question him, I tiptoed back to Cap's room and drifted off surprisingly fast. I've never been a good sleeper. A gift from Germain. Rarely a night passed without his hands on me. If I was lucky, it was only sex he was looking for. On other, not so lucky nights, it was my pain he sought.

"You're trembling. Do you want me to leave?"

"No." I wrap my arm over his, holding it tight. His hand splayed across my abdomen is so big he could tease both my nipples with little effort.

Ohmygod! I did not just think that.

I shudder, and heat pools in a place I haven't felt in longer than I can remember. My libido has been nonexistent. Now it rears its little head?

His hold tightens; his nose and mouth skim my shoulder. "I got you."

My nipples harden and tingle, my breath quickens. Oh, God. What the hell is wrong with me? I've never responded to a man's touch like this. He's not even trying to arouse me, but still, I am.

And it's so unfamiliar, I'm shaking like I'm scared, only this feels so different. So good.

His warmth seeps into my bones. His hard body is molded to mine like I was made to fit right here in his embrace. Another full-body shudder.

Stop! I chastise my body for choosing this moment to wake the heck up.

He only wants to be friends, and despite all evidence to the contrary, I'm pretty sure I'm not capable of more.

His hand flexes right under my breasts. Does he know? Can he sense it?

My pelvis tilts, pushing my ass back into him. *No!*

I swear he pushes back. I forget how to breathe for a minute. Is this what want feels like? Desire?

"Cher?" The graveled ring to my name has my back arching. Is that his cock? Is he hard? Why does that turn me on even more?

I've soaked my panties. I've never done that. I've read about it, but—

"Tell me what you need, baby."

Oh, God. I could never—

"Anything." His opened-mouth kiss to my neck has me shooting out of bed, stifling a moan and nearly bashing my injured head against the wall as my foot gets caught in the covers.

"Christ Almighty, Cher." He captures me around the waist, stopping my momentum, bringing me back to the bed with him on top of me, his hardness pressed to my core.

I blink at him in shock of his speed and agility and how he managed to get me back in bed without hurting my head.

"You alright?" He scans my face, his hand cupping my cheek.

"Did I do that to you? Or did you come to me with an erection?" What the fuck is wrong with me? I duck, waiting for the first strike to land.

Instead, he laughs so hard the bed shakes. I open my eyes to find his dimpled grin and warm eyes focused solely on me. He kisses my nose. "You're unexpected. I love the things that fly out of your mouth when you're not wound tight and afraid."

My brows nearly leave my forehead as I stare at him in wonder. "Really? Cause it's a new affliction." I've no clue what's wrong with me. I can't keep my mouth in check around him. "Maybe I have brain damage."

He runs his fingertips across my forehead. "Does your head hurt?"

"No." I'm having a hard time feeling anything besides the throbbing between my legs.

"Does your cut hurt?" He slides a hand down my body to still my hips that are mindlessly grinding against him.

When did *that* start?

Jeez, what he must think. "No."

He nods and licks his lips. "Does your pussy ache?"

"Ohmygod," I groan. I cannot believe he just said that. So cavalier, like talking about my p… is normal conversation.

He smiles softly. "I'm rock hard, Cher, because you were in my arms, pressed against me, fitting me so perfectly, and smelling like sweet nectar when you became aroused."

I cover my face. "Kill me now." I've never been so embarrassed.

He pries my hands away, trailing kisses along my jaw. "I'd rather make you come. Would you let me?"

What? Panic flares. He? What if… "I can't… I've never…" I want to crawl inside myself and die. I can't take his focus. His kindness. He's confusing me, and my body is on the fritz. "Please, don't."

"Fuck, I'm sorry. I never meant to…" He rolls to his back, pulling me into his side. "Sleep, Cher."

I curl into him, my head resting on his chest. "I'm sorry—"

"Don't. You've nothing to apologize for." He kisses my head. "We'll get there when you're ready."

79

I've no idea where *there* is. But the need to sleep hits me hard. His warmth, the beat of his heart, and the smell of serenity have me drifting off before I can second-guess or think I should be sleeping in a guestroom instead of here in the arms that could never be mine.

I'm broken into far too many pieces even for a saint of a man like James.

CAP

If I'm interpreting her words and reaction from last night correctly, Cher is a forty-two-year-old woman who was married longer than she's been single, has two kids, and has never had an orgasm.

My want to pin her to the kitchen counter and lick her until she comes on my tongue over and over again battles with the need to track down her asshole ex and annihilate him, slowly and painfully.

She's avoided all eye contact since she woke up still plastered to my chest. She slept that way all night. I didn't mind one bit. In fact, it's the best sleep I remember having as an adult.

Her family is coming over in a few hours. I've got brisket, ribs, and chicken smoking on the grill. Even though I haven't been home since before Vera gave birth to her third child, I still consider myself a Texan through and through. And as a Texan, we love to grill or smoke our meat.

Cher's working on the potato salad. I'm washing and trimming the green beans to steam at the last minute after the corn on the cob is done.

Before I let any more time go by, I address the tension that's been growing since we woke up. "Cher?"

"Hmm?" Her head down, mixing the potato salad, she barely acknowledges me.

"I'd like to talk about last night."

Her hand stills. "What part, exactly?"

I grab a fork from the drawer to the right of her hip and taste the potato salad. "Damn, that's good." I fork another bite and hold it out to her.

She eyes it, then me like I'm holding a dead snake in my hand.

"Trust me, Cher." I'd never trick her or do anything to purposefully cause her pain or embarrassment. "You're the one who made it."

On a single nod, she takes the bite, chews and smiles. "Good."

"It is." I don't just mean the food either.

"It'll be better tomorrow. I should have made it yesterday."

"You had a bit going on. Let it chill a while in the fridge. It'll be perfect." I cover the bowl with clear wrap and set it in the fridge. When I turn, I'm surprised to see her eyes on me. My heart thumps so loud, I'm sure she can hear it or see it beating through my shirt. "Cher, I don't want to be just friends."

Her eyes widen. "I-I thought you wanted to talk about last night."

I corral her to the counter and lift her up. "It's all a part of the same conversation." I lean in, rub my nose along hers. She sucks in air but doesn't pull away. I take that as a good sign. "I want to love on you. Show you what we can be like."

Her blues shimmer with uncertainty. "I don't know how—"

"I know. We'll take it slow and easy. There's no rush. No timetable. I like being with you. I want more of this"—I motion between us—"and a lot of this"—I gently press my lips to hers. Soft, tender, patient, all the things I've never considered myself being, but with her, I can do it—I'm willing to try.

And with her it feels easy.

Easier. Hell, I want this woman.

I never thought I'd want more with a woman again. But when she called me yesterday instead of the police or her son, the fear in her voice ripped through my callused heart, reminded me how fleeting life can be. I realized I was missing out on knowing her—especially if I never saw her again. I don't want to spend the rest of my life alone, and I sure as fuck don't want her to do the same.

"Be vulnerable with me, Cher. Let me in, and I promise to do the same. I'm a rusty, middle-aged man who wants to be needed by you."

"Cap." She pulls me in, hugging me tight.

"Need me, Cher. Cause I sure as hell need you."

CHAPTER 15

CHER

HAS ANYONE EVER SAID THEY NEED ME? MY kids needed me when they were younger. That didn't go so well. I let them down horribly. As an adult—I've never been needed before. The bloom in my chest warms me from the inside out. I take a deep drink of iced tea and refill my glass.

I told him I needed time to process what he was asking of me. He seemed so sure, so genuine. It's not a trick, right? I'm not going to say *yes*, and then he'll laugh in my face, telling me how stupid I am for thinking he could ever care for a *used-up cunt* like me.

Germaine, get out of my head. You too, Tom!

Wincing from the messed-up conversation in my head, I slip out of the kitchen and into the hall, taking a few steps away from the noise of my family, a minute to find my footing.

James is not Germaine.

James is not Tom.

"Mom?" Gabriel's comforting hand lands on my back as he comes into view. "You okay?"

No? I don't know if I ever was. I don't remember a time where I felt safe, secure, for more than a few fleeting moments at a time. I meet the honest gaze of my oldest. He's so handsome it makes my heart ache, but this newly freed tender side of him brings tears to my eyes. He should have been safe to be this man too.

He frowns. It's been a while since I've seen my boy's scowl—the one he's earned and worn so easily for most of his life—until Frankie. "What is it?" Concern riddles those three simple words.

"He's a good man, right?" The shake in my voice is unsettling and speaks to the importance of the answer to that question.

"Who?" He glances over my shoulder. "Hey, Cap."

"Cher? You alright?"

My gaze falls to Gabriel's chest. James deserves better than me. What could a shattered, ghost of a woman have to offer him?

Gabriel squeezes my arm, leans down to kiss my cheek and whispers, "Yeah, Mom. He's the best. The real deal." He leaves the two of us alone.

Seconds later I'm pulled into James' chest. "I've upset you."

I hold him tight, wanting to believe what my heart is telling me. "I think I was born upset, James. Don't take it personally."

He chuckles and tips my chin. "I think the world had a thing or two to do with that, Cher." He runs his palm along my cheek, his gaze so tender. "You come to me when you're upset. Even if I'm the cause, I promise to hold you until it's better or let you berate me until you feel better. Whatever you need, Plum. Let me be it."

"God." My forehead hits his chest. "I want to believe you."

"Trust. I need to earn it. I get it." He kisses my head. "Give me a chance. That's all I ask."

Bravery I doubt I have lifts my face to his. "Why? Why me? You like your women broken, Cap?" I regret the implications as soon as the harsh words fall from my lips.

His chest rumbles as he picks me up and stomps down the hall.

Closing the door to his office, he sets me on my feet, steps away and paces to the wall and back. "Don't," he seethes. "Don't talk about yourself like that. I won't stand for it." He huffs, turns and paces again, his hands digging in his hair.

Something's wrong. No, not wrong.

Something's... right?

If he were Germain, I'd be shaking and begging him for forgiveness. It dawns on me then... "I'm not scared."

James turns and faces me. "What?"

I point at him. "I've obviously upset you. You're angry." My hand drops to my side. "I'm not afraid. You won't hurt me even though you're mad."

His shoulders fall. "No. Fuck. Of course, I won't hurt you."

"No," I hold up my hand, "you're missing my point. I'm. Not. Scared."

In two strides my face is locked between his massive hands. "You're saying you're not afraid of me?"

No. "I know you won't hit me."

He growls, but it's in frustration over my past and not at me. "Never."

"I have a hard time believing out of all the woman in your world, Cap, that you'd want a mess like me."

"Cher," he warns.

"I mean it. I know you could have any woman out there... normal... with so much less baggage. Why me?"

He shrugs. "Don't know." He sits and pulls me between his legs. "I've only loved one woman, Cher. She broke my heart in so many pieces, I never wanted or even tried to find love again. What you witnessed in my office so many years ago, was my life—has been my life since the Marine Corps." He kisses my hand, closes his eyes and holds it to his lips. "There's something about you. There always has been. I've fought it. But hearing the fear in your voice yesterday, the possibility that things could have gone so wrong, made me realize I don't want to live the rest of my life never loving again... Never loving *you*."

"James." He can't...

"I'm not saying... It's just... I see a future for the first time when I look in your eyes—and I want it. Broken or not, Cher, I only want you." He pulls me down, his lips a hair's breadth from mine. "Give this old dog a bone—give me a chance."

"You're not old. You're only a year older than me."

"My creaking joints beg to differ."

"That's only because you're not eating the right—"

"Don't talk about food unless you're going to feed me those lips."

"I—"

"Now, Cher—"

I slam my mouth to his, not gracefully, not seductively. What do I know about either of those things? He cups the sides of my face, his fingers gently touching the back of my head, not hurting my cut, just holding me close, guiding as his mouth traverses mine. His tongue slips in with no resistance from me. His full lips are soft and taste like the chocolate cake he stole a bite of earlier—sinfully delicious and decadent. So, this is what heaven tastes like?

"Christ Almighty, woman," he breathes across my lips. "I could eat you for breakfast, lunch, and dinner."

"Oh." I squirm on his lap.

He stills me with a grip on my hip. "You should go before I do something stupid like fuck you into tomorrow with your family in the other room."

Ohmygod. I close my eyes on a moan as want rushes to my core. He doesn't treat me like I'm broken. He treats me like... He *wants* me.

"Fuck, Cher. You look like you need me to do just that."

"Maybe I do?"

He sighs, kisses my forehead and sets me on my feet. "Go. I'll be there in a minute." He adjusts his massive hard-on in his jeans.

"I—"

"Go." He squeezes my hand and offers a gentle smile. "I'll be there shortly."

I leave him to deal with his... affliction. I've never been sent away when a man was still hard. I was always a tool to alleviate the ache. First my father, then Germain. I've never been allowed to walk away unscathed.

Unused.

Who is this man? He must be a saint, for he's like no man I've ever known.

And that kiss... I burn for more.

CHAPTER 16

CAP

"YOU ALRIGHT, REESE?" I GLANCE OVER Reese's shoulder to Cher loving on Ox and smile. She's a good grandmother despite all her doubts about being a good mother. She raised two great kids under horrible circumstances. She's an abused woman, not a soldier who's trained to fight back. I don't know if anyone could have done better.

"Yeah." Reese fiddles with the cap of her bottled water. She's not okay.

"I'm sorry Rowdy didn't come." Is that what's got her out of sorts? I know she's not crazy about socializing, but she's done so well at the gym, and this is family.

"Hmm." She nods, backing up. "I'm gonna check out the swing." She scurries away before I can stop her.

"She thinks Rowdy isn't here because of her." Frankie plops down next to me on the couch. Her eyes trail Gabriel as he stands watching his sister through the window.

Really? "What do you think?"

She shrugs. "I don't know. He's been distant since Gabriel and I got back together, but I thought things were better after Maddox was born. But then he lost his mom…" The worry in her eyes hits me hard.

"He just needs time, Frankie. He asked you to marry him. He was willing to give you all his tomorrows."

"You think—"

"No. He loves Reese. He's just messed up over seeing you with the baby that he offered to raise as his own, then he lost his mom. He just needs time to find his way." I wrap her in a hug. "You're a good momma, Frankie. I'm so proud of you."

She groans my name, swiping at her eyes. My girl's a tough one, but she's learning to let her emotions free now that she's found peace and safety with Gabriel.

Maybe the hormones are contributing a little?

"Shh… Let me have a fatherly second."

The man I love like a son stomps over, narrowing his eyes on me. "You making my Angel cry, old man?"

"Just sharing my fatherly pride is all." I loosen my grip, knowing he's about to pull her out of my grasp, anyway.

His face softens. "That'll do it." He kisses her forehead. "I'm going outside to talk to Ree. You okay?" The tenderness he shows as he catches her last tear is admirable.

"I'm proud of you too, Gabriel." He's come so far from the angry teen he was when I first met him.

His gaze swivels to me, and he whispers, "You catch feelings for my mom, and now you're all sentimental?" He smirks and puts a finger over Frankie's lips before she can voice her shock. "Don't say anything, Angel. She's skittish." His fierce gaze is back on me. "You got that, right?"

More importantly… "I've got her."

"Good man." He kisses Frankie again. "I'll be back." He kisses his mom and Ox on his way out the back door.

"You've been good for him," I say, watching him pass by the window toward the porch swing at the corner of the deck. "The boy I met, and the man I welcomed home from the Army, never would have shown so much affection or talked about it so freely."

"I could say the same about you."

I smile down at her before my gaze sweeps across the room to Cher rocking Ox in the rocking chair I bought for that very reason. "Things are falling into place."

"Are they?" I hear the question in her voice.

"Do you know why the military is so tough on new recruits? You have to break someone down to build them back up the way they were always meant to be."

"Weed out the flaws?"

"To make them stronger." I turn my eyes back to her. "If you'd met Gabriel at fourteen instead of Austin, would you have the kind of love you have now?"

"God, no." She grimaces at the thought. "We wouldn't have been ready for each other."

I chuckle at her reaction. "You've been to battle, Frankie. You can appreciate the peace, the sacrifice it took to get here. But you're also a better person for your hardships and strife."

"And Cheryl?" she whispers.

"She's been put back together perfectly. She fits me, Frankie. Just the way she is. You okay with that?"

"Yeah, there's just a lot of… baggage."

"We've all got it. Some more than others. She needs someone, and I want it to be me."

"But does she *want* that?"

"That's the million-dollar question now, isn't it?"

I've barely brushed my teeth and am about to slip into bed where I sent Cher a few hours ago, when I hear a racket at the front door. Pulling on my t-shirt and workout pants, I silently make my way downstairs.

Swinging the door open, I'm surprised to find Gabriel and Rowdy swaying, holding each other up. "Jesus. Tell me you two are not drunk on my front porch at this time of night?" Did they drive like this? Granted they're both only a few blocks away, but still.

"My family get home okay?" Gabriel spouts as he stops their spin to face me.

I school my embarrassment of him knowing his mom might still be here in my bed. Though we haven't had sex, like he might assume, it's still awkward as fuck.

Of course, I got Frankie and Ox home hours ago after Gabriel left unexpectedly to go see Rowdy. I just didn't expect them to show up here. "Come on in before you fall over." I move back to ensure they don't run me over. Between the two of them, they weigh over five hundred pounds. I don't want that landing on me.

With Gabriel practically passed out on my couch, I sit Rowdy at my kitchen table and fill him with coffee and chocolate cake, wondering if I should have made him that sandwich he said *yes* to.

When I tell him Reese already had some of the chocolate cake he just offered to take to her, he sobers. "She did?" His light eyes shine with so much sadness. "I should have been here."

"Yep, you should have. Why weren't you?"

"You."

"Me?" I don't take offense. He's drunk.

I work on making up his coffee the way I know he likes it, switch and duplicate the process. He takes it just like I do. "Why am I the reason you didn't come?" When he doesn't answer I ask again, "Why didn't you come today?"

"Did you know a Vera Orlena Permian-O'Dair?"

What?! I choke on my coffee, spitting it across the table. "Fuck." I work on clean-up as my mind races. Why the hell would he ask me that? Ask me about *her*? Fuck. Why, Vera? Why do you insist on haunting me even after all these years? Just when I'm about to move on. "How do you know that name?"

"She was my mother."

"W-what?" I pop to my feet, knocking my chair over. That's not possible. He can't... Fuck, I can't breathe. "Vera was your mom?" *Your mom who died?*

"Yes," he croaks as if telling me hurts as bad as me feeling the punch of his words.

Christ Almighty. Vera, God, no. I study his face, his features. She's... Vera is gone? She's dead? The punch keeps stinging. I cover my mouth to stifle the cry that escapes. I turn to save any dignity I have left, but it's useless as wave after wave of regret and remorse pummel me.

Vera is dead. *My Vera.*

"Did you love her?" Rowdy approaches, my anguish reflecting back in his eyes. "Did you love my mom?"

More than my next breath, at times. "I didn't mean to, but God help me, I did." I tried not to.

Silently he drinks down his coffee that can't be cool enough to chug like he is.

"That's why you didn't come? Because you found out I knew your mom?" It's a good reason. I can understand if he feels differently about me knowing I had a relationship with his mom.

How the hell did he find me or I find him?

I move closer when he doesn't answer. "Rowdy?"

He shakes his head as if to dispel whatever's in there fighting to get out. His struggle is real. Palpable. It's eating him up inside. This is why he hasn't been coming to the gym? Why he's pulled away from us—from me.

"Rowdy." I need the truth, and he needs to unburden himself.

"No, that's not why I didn't come tonight." His pain guts me.

I crowd him, pushing him to let it go. "Tell me."

Nearly nose to nose, our gazes locked, he admits, "I didn't come because I found out my dad is not my dad. *You* are."

No. I crumple to my knees. Years of regret and useless sacrifice fall around me, stifling the air and making it hard to breathe.

CHAPTER 17

CAP

CHRIST ALMIGHTY. FIRST VERA. NOW THIS. HOW much more?

"I'm sorry, Cap." Rowdy sniffles. He's torn up. Of course he is. "I wish there was an easier way to tell you. I wish we'd known."

He's mine. This gentle giant is mine?

Vera gave me a son. We created a son... Together.

I have a son?

I know this young man well, and he's *mine*?

A new wave of anguish hits me.

His strong hand lands on my back. I fight for control, but fuck, the vise around my heart hurts like hell as the last of the love a part of me kept deep inside for Vera bleeds out.

She gave me a son. All these years, she lied to me. Barrett lied to me. My boy's been right under my nose for nearly a year, and I never saw it. I wish...

"Uh, Cap. I don't mean to make this worse, but I feel I should tell you the rest. Not drag it out."

Christ. "Fuck, there's more?" I wipe at my tears, suck in as much air as I can muster, and meet his gaze over my shoulder. The color of his eyes are not mine, but they are so familiar. Fuck. Me. How did I not see it before? "Cameron..." I sit back. She didn't. "Jesus."

"What?"

"Your name. Cameron is *my* middle name." I fight to breathe, managing to get a few stifled breaths.

A light goes on in his eyes. "They named me after you."

"So they did." Remembering his words, there's more. "What's the rest of the news?"

"You've got a daughter. My younger sister. Taylor is yours too."

What the actual fuck? I squeeze my eyes shut. My head hits the counter. The knocks just keep coming.

I have a daughter. *Fuck. I have a daughter.*

What did you do, Vera? Did you plan it? Was I simply a stud to you? Did our time together mean nothing to you? Wham bam, thank you, ma'am, now get out of my life?

Barrett allowed this? The man who barely claims me as his half-brother—hates me—yet he raised my kids and named one after me?

God. Rowdy. What he's been going through, dealing with this. I turn to see my son's eyes locked on me, waiting. "I'm sorry, Rowdy. I just need a minute here."

"No." He shakes his head. "I get it. I've known for weeks, and I'm still fucked up over it."

A few seconds pass before he stands and helps me to my feet. "I don't expect anything from you, Cap. You've already done a lot for me. But this was a secret I could no longer carry. I'm sorry for dumping it on you like this."

I knew the minute I spotted Rowdy he was a good kid—a good man. He had the misfit gene about him, besides his talent, that *thing* that just drew me to him. That *thing* that told me he'd fit. He'd appreciate my family, appreciate the chance to further his MMA career, but also be a part of something bigger than himself.

He's fucking *mine*.

All this time. Did I sense it? Did I know? Fuck. Fuck. Fuck. I pull him into me, forehead to forehead. "You did right by telling me. We'll figure this out." *Jesus, fuck, Vera.* "I just need a minute." Way fucking more than a minute, but he doesn't need to see me losing my shit more than he already has. He's shown such strength. It's the least I can do—be strong too.

"Yep." His gaze falls behind me. "I should get Gabriel home to his family."

I turn to find my son by choice standing there, raw emotions in his eyes. "Thanks for getting him over here, Gabriel."

"Sure, Cap." Gabriel hauls me into a hug, bringing Rowdy in too. I latch on tight, drawing strength from these formidable men I'm lucky to know, much less call family—sons.

"This is y'all's business," Gabriel's gruff voice breaches the silence. "Frankie and I are here for whatever you need. But don't think for one second this isn't a blessing in disguise."

I have children—by blood. I've considered Gabriel and Frankie my kids for a long time now. I always have room for more, but how will they feel about it? Gabriel doesn't seem threatened by the notion. Will Frankie? She loves Rowdy. Hell, she almost married him. These three, so tightly bound by their Frankie connection and what might have beens. Turns out they're all mine. I pray they see it as a plus, not a competition—or worse. Blood or not, they're mine.

I swallow back more tears. *Fuck, Cher, I need you.*

Gabriel looks to my son by blood. "Rowdy, you just lost your mom but gained a father."

Tight-jawed, fighting to keep it together, Rowdy just nods on a grunt.

Gabriel squeezes my shoulder. "Cap, you're like the father Frankie and I never had. You're a good, kind-hearted man who should've been a father all along. Turns out you were—you just didn't know it. Take whatever time you need. But know the guys will support you all the way if y'all decide to let it be known."

Christ, do I tell the guys? Will they be happy about this? Will they feel threatened or worry about favoritism? They should all know me better than that by now.

Gabriel pats me on the back. "See you outside," he says to Rowdy.

Rowdy pulls an envelope out of his back pocket. "I got a letter from my mom. This was inside it." He hands it to me. "It's for you."

Can I stand to read Vera's last words to me?

I'm shamefully silent when Rowdy leaves. I should have said more. Done more.

I just... need a minute.

CHER

Quietly, I descend the stairs to find James slouched on the couch, staring into space, hands at his sides, and a piece of paper loosely held in one hand.

Should I leave him alone? If it were my father or Germain, I'd never have come looking—I'd have likely gotten punched in my nose for poking it where it didn't belong. But this is James. Even if he's mad at me for prodding, he's hurting right now.

Is that what a good partner would do? We're more than friends... If it were my kids, I would approach them and see what I could do to make it better. Deciding that's the right course of action, I move forward.

He doesn't move or flinch. He's barely blinking. The closer I get, the harder I focus on his sad, reddened eyes and the pinch in his jaw. Approaching an upset man has never gone well for me.

When his eyes flash to me, I jump and freeze in place. But his one-word plea, "Cher," shatters the unease and has me climbing into his lap and holding him as tight as I can.

He wraps around me, his head buried in my neck. "Did you hear?"

"A little. I tried not to. I'm sorry."

"No, it's fine. I just didn't know how much you knew or what I needed to share."

"You want to tell me?" I'm ashamed of the shock in my voice. Most people don't think to tell me anything. I'm an afterthought at best, forgotten at the worst. He said he wanted me vulnerable, wanted me to trust him, and he'd do the same.

And… He's actually doing it.

My heart trips over itself, galloping at full speed toward him. He sees me. He needs me. Me. I never saw that coming.

He holds the piece of paper out to me. "It's from Vera."

I take it but keep my eyes on him. "Vera?"

"The woman I loved," he catches my chin when I start to look away, "a long time ago. I just found out she's Rowdy's mother… And, well, read for yourself."

I can't believe he's willing to share something so personal with me. Wait. Rowdy's mother died. This letter has to be intensely personal. "You sure?"

He motions to the letter. "Read."

Dear Jimmy,

I'm sorry you found out this way. I'm sorry I'm not here to soothe your ruffled feathers. You're going to hate me, if you don't already. It's hard to believe it's been eighteen years since I've seen your handsome face, since I've been loved by the strongest, bravest man I've ever known.

Gah, she *knew* him… *Loved* him… *Recognized* what a wonderful man he is. I meet James' teary-eyed gaze. "I'm sorry." My chin wobbles as I try to hold it together. It's so personal and devastating. I'm still in shock he wants to share something so personal with me. *Me.*

"Read, Cher." He kisses my hand and settles me against his chest. I can feel him reading along with me as I continue.

Dang, this is going to hurt, isn't? Dredging up the past to heal old wounds and open up new ones you didn't even know existed. I'm sorry for that too, but give this dying woman a moment to tell you her side of the story...

I fell hard for you. Harder than you ever thought, especially when I married Barrett. You broke my heart when you joined the Marines. It's not like I didn't know it was your plan all along. I knew. I'd hoped you'd choose me instead. It was immature and naïve of me, but we were eighteen. What are you if not naive and immature at that age? You left to become the man you thought you needed to become. I know you left because of your family too. And me marrying Barrett only solidified your reasons for staying away. I'm so sorry for that—for being the wedge that kept you from ever having a relationship with your brother.

Holy... "She married your brother?"

"Yep."

Wow. I hate her just a little bit. A lot a bit. Sorry, Rowdy.

I was selfish. I didn't think I was strong enough to wait for you to come home, or chance being alone in the event you didn't—or decided you no longer wanted me. So instead, I married your brother, knowing it would hurt you. It was also the only way I could keep a part of you with me always—at least that's what I thought at the time.

Then you came home on leave. We connected. Then you left again. I found out I was pregnant a month later. I knew the baby was yours without a doubt because Barrett hadn't touched me since Drake was born. Don't get me wrong. Barrett was a good husband. He loved me in his own way. He just wasn't a physically affectionate man. He loved me in other ways. Ways I learned to live with. Ways that didn't involve sex.

I was elated about the pregnancy. I was happy for the first time in such a long time, knowing I would have a piece of you with me always. I loved Rowdy with all the love I had for you. He's always been the light of my life, my fierce boy who's so much like his father.

What?! "Y-you're Rowdy's father?"

As a tear slips down his cheek, he answers through a clenched jaw, "Yes."

"You didn't know?"

Big, heart-wrenching tears fall. "I had no idea." The break in his voice does me in.

I lunge, holding him so tight, I fear I might break him or me. "I'm so sorry. That's horrible." And so, so sad. I can't imagine never knowing Gabriel or Reese.

The devastation in his cries rips me up inside, but also elevates him beyond his already god-like status. Captain James Durant is a tough, stone-hard warrior with a heart of gold. I'm ashamed I doubted him—his words. He is who he says he is. Integrity runs through his veins, and though he hasn't been *in love* in years, he loves hard. He loves Gabriel and Frankie like they were his own. He's always been a father, if not by blood, by choice. But now, he's both.

Only, he's missed out on so much. "I can't image the hurt and anger you're feeling, but believe this—finding out he's yours is a good thing. Rowdy is a good man—just like his father."

He crushes the last of the air out of my lungs. I don't care. I'd gladly die to bring this man a moment's peace.

"Read," he croaks, pulling away, drying his face. "There's more."

More? Can I handle more? How did *he* handle more?

My heart breaks at the thought of him reading this alone.

I have kids. I raised them, but I was never the mother they deserved. He has kids, but didn't know. He's definitely the father they deserve—or should want. Anyone should consider themselves blessed to be under Cap's protection, on his radar, in his universe. I don't deserve him. But maybe if I try to be a better mom, I'll be close to deserving a man like James.

He may not have judged me for the poor mother I was, but now that he knows he's a father, will that change? I pray not.

I adjust to hold the letter so we can both continue reading.

I never thought I'd be so blessed or loved again by you, but then you came home one last time—only I didn't know it was the last time. You've given me more joy than you can ever know. First Rowdy, then Taylor, your daughter. If you can't guess, I named her after our favorite singer, James Taylor, because you shared a first name with him, I gave her his last. You used to sing to me. Do you remember? So many nights in your arms listening to you sing his songs. Do you still sing? Do you still play? Taylor loves music, just like you did. She's fierce and protective like you too.

I wish I could tell you I kept them from you for a good reason, but the truth is, I was selfish. Barrett stayed with me, knowing they were yours. He promised to raise them as his own, but I had to promise not to tell you. Not to tell them. That's not on him. It's on me for not being strong enough to suffer the consequences of telling the truth. I guess I'm suffering now for keeping the secret. Maybe the lies ate at my insides, created the cancer.

This is my punishment—missing out on their future. I got to raise them. Now, you get to see them through the rest of their lives. Maybe it will give you some solace knowing I've suffered for my deceit. I never did it to hurt you.

I don't have to ask you to let them in—to love them—as I know you already care for our son. I've no doubt when the time is right, you will have a place for Taylor in your heart as well. I wrote her a letter. Barrett has it. I don't know when he plans on giving it to her, but I hope for her sake it's soon. She deserves to know a man like you, have you set the example for how a man should treat a woman.

This brings me to the end of my confessions, but not the end of my love. I loved two men in my life, not equally, not fairly, but deeply all the same. You were never meant for me. You may believe otherwise, but I give you this: If you were my one and only, you wouldn't have been able to leave me so easily, and I wouldn't have been able to love your brother.

If you ever find your other half, don't let her go. Reese is Rowdy's Wendy (he'll explain). Now let me go, Jimmy. Forgive me. Love our kids. Let me lie in peace knowing they're in your hands. And for the love of God, or me, love again. Find your Belle, the one who soothes the ache in your chest, the hole in your heart, the only one who can tame the Beast in you.

My unwavering love and respect,
Vera

Silently, he carries me upstairs, crawls in bed and holds me until his breathing deepens and the scowl on his face softens into restful sleep. The tracks of his tears, long dried on his face, shimmer in the moonlight.

"I want to be your Belle," I whisper into the dark, not believing it's possible, or knowing everything that means to him, but wanting it all the same.

CHAPTER 18

CAP

MORNING HITS LIKE A TON OF BRICKS. GROGGY, I sit up, legs over the edge of the bed, my head in my hands. If I didn't know the reason for my pounding headache, I'd think I went on a bender last night. An emotional hangover is just as bad. Maybe worse.

I have kids, my conscience reminds me.

Cher. I swing around only to freeze at the sight of her side of the bed empty and made up like she didn't sleep with me last night.

She did, didn't she?

"Fuck." I scrub my face and head for the bathroom. Thank God it's Sunday. A day to get my life in order before Monday comes knocking.

After a quick shower, I'm rejuvenated and determined to track down one missing Plum. She could be downstairs, but I'm fairly certain she ran, hard, and fast. My baggage a little too much for her. Maybe. I intend on finding out.

In the car, I call Rowdy.

"Morning, Cap." Sounds like I just woke him.

"Sorry if I woke you."

"No, just dragging a little. That damn chocolate cake." He yawns.

I chuckle and fight the need to yawn too. "Yeah, it was the cake that got you and not the whisky… or the emotions."

"You okay?" The fact he can even ask me that after everything he's found out, points to the kind-hearted man he is.

He's mine. Fuck. It hits me all over again.

How'd I get so lucky? Vera and Barrett did me wrong by not telling me, but still, I'm blessed to have him now.

"I'm good. I was wondering if you were free for, say, dinner or something."

"Sure." Not even a moment's hesitation. "I'm taking Reese to my place this morning. You want to come for dinner, around sixish?"

"Sounds perfect."

"Reese will be there."

I assumed so. "Sounds even better." I've nothing to hide, other than my growing attraction and frustration with her mother. "See you soon."

"Yep. Bye."

I swing by for coffee and food before traipsing up to Cher's door, pounding like the damn door did me wrong.

Pounding on her door is becoming a habit.

The startle on her face has me slowing my roll, but not the censure in my tone. "You left. You snuck out."

She smiles. She fucking smiles, and damn if my heart doesn't do a happy dance.

"You're mad." She's still fucking smiling. She's happy about that?

"Yeah, Plum. I liked the idea of waking up with you in my arms."

Her smile grows into a full-blown toothy grin. Christ Almighty, my heart.

"Do you want to come in?" she asks as she steps back.

I want to do a hell of a lot more than that, but it's a start. "Yes, please."

She dips her head as I pass, hiding her pleasure from me. Not happening. I want it all.

Setting down the coffee and bag of food on the kitchen island, I grip her around the waist and set her next to them. "Don't do that." I lose all sanity in her blue-as-fuck eyes, so brilliant in the morning light coming through the windows. Are Gabriel's and Reese's this blue? Can't be.

"Don't do what?" She bites her lip to stop her smile.

"Don't sneak out on me. I don't like it. I don't like it one bit. You come to bed with me, you be there in the morning unless we've discussed otherwise. Or leave a note, for fuck's sake." My heart cracks on the effervescent smile that breaks free, making her look more beautiful than I've ever seen her—no makeup and all. "What's up with the smiling, Cher? I'm upset here, and you're not taking me seriously."

She grips my shirt, frowning.

Now I miss her smile, and I'm pissed I made it disappear. What the fuck's wrong with me?

"I am. I swear. It's just…"

"Tell me." I'm losing patience.

"You're mad at me."

My brow shoots up. "And that makes you smile?" There's something wrong here.

"I thought yesterday was a fluke, when you got mad and nothing happened. But you're mad again. You're not holding back, not treating me with kid gloves."

Frowning, I lean in, nose to nose. "Is that a good thing? Because I'm not exactly sure of the right answer here."

She smooshes my cheeks in her perfect little hands. "It's a good thing. You're mad and not taking it out on me physically—that's a great thing. I feel safe—"

I crash my mouth to hers. Too much fucking talking. Her sultry moan has me groaning and hardening in my jeans, my tongue slipping in to dance with hers. And damn if she isn't an amazing dancer.

When her grip on my shoulders tightens, I pull back, catching a full breath. "Breakfast." I nod to the bag next to her. "We need to eat." *Before I lay you out and eat you.*

CHER

Kissing James puts all kinds of ideas in my head. I'm a bit lost in them and the breakfast he brought over when a knock on the door makes me jump in my seat.

James' hand lands on mine. "I'll get it."

I stand in the kitchen entry, watching him stalk to the door, larger than life. If I didn't know for a fact that Gabriel fit through my doors, I'd doubt James could. With agile confidence, he manages just fine. He swings open the door without even checking the peephole.

Out of habit, I move to warn him, but slink back and bite my tongue. He can take care of himself. He doesn't need my protection—not like I *could* protect him.

"Cher." James' eyes meet mine over his shoulder. He holds out his hand, calling me to him.

I stop short when Tom comes into view, standing on the other side of the threshold.

Cap faces me, whispering, "He can't hurt you, Plum. I'm here. He has something he wants to say, but I'll send him away if you don't care to hear it. You say the word."

My gaze bounces between the two. James doesn't seem the least bit unsettled by Tom's appearance. I can't say the same.

Did Cap know Tom was coming?

Hesitantly, I move closer to the door. James pulls me into his side.

"Cheryl—"

James growls.

"—Ms. Stone," Tom corrects himself. "I'm sorry for what happened the other day. I was out of line for..." His eyes jump to James and back. "...all of it. I was completely in the wrong."

I think Tom is actually shaking in his boots—I glance down—dress shoes. His nervousness eases mine. There's no way James would let Tom get close enough to lay a hand on me.

"...I don't expect you to forgive me." He hands me a thick envelope. "But I hope this will serve as restitution for my behavior, lost income, and distress I've caused you."

Astonished, all I can do is blink and process this strange turn of events.

He fumbles on, "I... uh, included a letter of reference, should you need it. You've been nothing but exemplary and professional in all our dealings." He eyes Cap again before awkwardly waving and walking backwards to his car.

We stand there, watching until he drives off. "Um, Cap, what did you do?"

He shuts the door, locking it. "What do you mean?"

"Really?" I point to the door. "Are you telling me you had nothing to do with that?"

He smiles and pulls me back to the kitchen. "I plead the fifth." He points to the table. "Please finish eating. It's getting cold."

I cross my arms over my chest and wait him out.

Sighing, he grips my hips and pulls me in. "You're a stubborn one, aren't you?" He kisses my neck, right on my thudding pulse. "I pointed out the error of his ways. Suggested he make financial restitution. That's all."

"Did you hurt him?"

He scowls. "Do you *really* care if I did? He hurt you, Cher. I won't stand by and let that go unanswered."

I soften for this big savior of a man. "I don't want you to get in trouble because of me."

His dimpled smile is hard to resist. "No trouble, I promise. Please eat. I'd like to take you somewhere."

Because I'm still hungry, I do as he asks, enjoying the view as he sits next to me, eating with his right hand and his left on my knee, not moving, just sitting there… Claiming.

I want to screech like a schoolgirl who just got asked out for the first time. But I'm not a schoolgirl. I'm a grown-ass woman, who's never known love or respect from a man. He has my head swimming with hope and my heart fluttering and banging against my chest to get to him.

CHAPTER 19

CHER

WE PULL UP TO THE NEW SHOPPING CENTER I've watched being built for the past few months. James brings his truck to a stop at the end of a cute corner shop. It's the only one with an extended patio area that's currently being sectioned off with a wrought iron fence.

He gets out without a word, comes around and opens my door.

"What are we doing here?"

He offers his hand. "Trust me, Cher. Hear me out."

That sets off alarm bells. I'm not big on surprises. But I take his hand and follow him inside the empty store, trusting, believing I'm safe with him.

Inside, the vision of what this barren space could be—a bakery—hits me. Four walls, unfinished, ready to be built out. It's big enough to accommodate a nice-sized kitchen, maybe an office, and plenty of room out front for display cases and seating. Plus, the outside patio. The scent of fresh-baked apple pie hits my senses…

"This is mine," he offers as explanation.

What? The fantasy fades. "This store?"

"No, this development." He moves to the windows and points down the way. "I've got a handful of chain stores lined up: household goods, a restaurant, a few clothing stores. They'll be the draw, but I want local business to fill the rest."

Sounds like a good plan. "Okay."

He turns to me. "This is your bakery, Cher. Sugarplum's."

"I'm sorry, what?!" I stumble back till I hit something solid.

James follows, his hand gripping my hip. "Breathe, baby."

Once I've taken a few solid breaths, he slips his hand in mine and starts to walk around. "It's completely up to you, but I see a kitchen in back. A wall with a swinging door dividing the back of the store from the front. A window between so you can see the customers as you bake—or they can see you working your magic…"

He proceeds to describe the place exactly as I envisioned it, as if I'd shared all those dreams with him instead of keeping them locked up for fear of being mocked for daring to think I could run a business on my own, for daring to want more for myself.

"What do you think?" We're back at the front of the store. He's staring at me expectantly.

"I think you're crazy." Everything he said is wonderful, but I could never afford this place. I have Tom's cash and some money saved but nowhere enough to open my own shop. Besides, opening any shop is a gamble—the money I have is actual security, so I'm not any more of a burden to my children than I have been—or maybe a little inheritance I can give them when I'm gone.

How could I gamble even a dollar of that away on a silly dream for myself?

"I'm crazy for you. I'm crazy for your sweets. Everyone is. You keep cooking what you know and love, the people will come. I know it." He's so confident it would succeed—like anything I touch wouldn't disintegrate the way it always has. But with him it's different—he makes things happen, makes them feel different. He makes me want things I didn't know I could want.

I'm sure I'm blushing from his praise. My face is burning. He reaches up and caresses my cheek with the back of his hand. "I want to help, Plum. Let me do this for you."

"What exactly are you offering?" I'm intoxicated by hearing about this version of me in his mind who can do things like open successful bakeries with zero experience. It doesn't hurt to hear him out, right?

"I own the place, so no rent. It's yours to do with as you wish. I can help you as much as you want with planning, running it, or I can be a silent partner with no say in anything. It's up to you."

"It's a great dream." I turn to the open space, already seeing the employees and customers mingling while I peek out from the kitchen, waiting on the timer to go off on the turnovers I have in the oven. "I can't afford this." Reality smashes the image before my eyes.

He blankets my back, circling my waist. "You can with my help and the money Tom gave you."

"I can't take your money. That's a surefire way to ruin a friendship."

He kisses the side of my neck and up to my ear. "Consider it an investment in your future—our future. You start making money, you pay me back. It'll be a success, Cher. I've no doubt."

I turn in his arms. "And what if this thing between us turns sour?"

He smiles wide and deep. "This thing between us is definitely going to turn, but it won't be sour, Plum." He steps back. "But let's talk it through." He holds up his right hand. "On one hand, you take me up on my offer, we get involved, fall in love, get married, have babies, live happily ever after."

"What?! Babies?" He's insane, plus I can't—

"Hear me out." He holds up his left hand. "On the other hand, you take me up on my offer. We crash and burn as a couple. We have a contract that protects you and your investment." His hands fall to his sides. "Gabriel is like a son to me, Frankie, my daughter, and Ox, my grandson.

I'm not going anywhere, Cher, and I have every intention of you and me working out. But this offer"—he motions around the room—"isn't tied to being in my bed or not." He steps into me, close but not touching. "It's a solid offer. You've got a whole family—my family—backing you. Your food is like crack. You can't fail unless you don't try."

CAP

She's quiet on the way to her place. I'm unsure if that's good or bad. She didn't come flat out and say *no*. I'll take it as a minor win.

The sheer disbelief on her face when I said *babies* was surprising. Though I hadn't really considered it until that very moment, I can envision having at least a baby or two with her. She's only forty-two. It's still possible. And though my joints ache like I'm old, I'm only a year older. There are lots of forty-something-year-olds having kids.

I said it off the cuff, but now the idea has stuck.

I missed Rowdy and Taylor growing up. For the first time ever, I regret the choice to not have kids. I would have gladly had them with Vera had we stayed together. But the idea of having them without her... I wasn't interested. Turns out I had two with her. I missed their birth, their first steps, their first words. I missed every. Fucking. Thing.

Fuck. I can't stop thinking about it. I want to meet Taylor. I believe Rowdy and I will be just fine. We'll continue on the same course we've been on since we met—except closer. Like Gabriel, he wedged in a little deeper than most. Now I know why.

My soul always knew he was mine.

I want to tell the world. Is he ready for that?

I'll find out tonight.

"I'm going to Rowdy's tonight. Reese will be there. Do you want to go with me?" I break the silence.

I'd love to have her by my side, but I have a feeling even if I hadn't brought up the bakery idea today, she wouldn't go. Cher is far from social. And her and Reese's relationship is strained, odd. They don't fight. They don't seem to dislike each other. It's more of a mutual ignoring. They're supportive of each other, but... They don't go out of their way to interact, but they don't go out of their way to avoid each other either. They're simply... existing.

She studies me for a long moment before answering, "No, but thank you."

"Is it because of today?"

Cher squeezes my forearm. "No. Your offer is more than generous and thoughtful. It's just... Reese wouldn't want me there."

Is she right? "Why?" If I don't ask, I'll never know. The Stones aren't big on sharing details of their past.

"She feels more herself when I'm not around." She says it so sure, without emotion, like it's a fact.

"Are you okay with that?"

She swings around. "You mean am I okay that my daughter can't stand to be in the same room with me?" She huffs out a puff of air. "Hardly."

"Would you change it if you could?" I side-eye her, gauging her reaction. Am I pushing her too far?

"I'd love to have a relationship with my daughter, but that's a selfish notion. She's been hurt irrevocably by my selfishness. I can't—won't—force anything on her. The type of relationship we have is her call. I'm here. Always... waiting." Her gaze drifts out the window.

Now I sense her sadness. So often she separated herself from the emotion of her past. I don't know many of the details of what Germain did to them other than severely beating on them and controlling—belittling Cher. I sense the damage Germain did to Cher and Reese is far worse. Whatever went down put a wedge between mother and daughter that neither of them are in any hurry to remove.

"Would you tell me about it?"

Her head whips around. "You want to know about Germain?"

"Yes."

She nods. "I suppose it's only fair, considering you should know who you might be getting into business with."

No. "Cher, your past has no impact on our business or personal relationship."

Head shaking, her focus slips back out the window. "You won't feel that way once you know the truth. I'm weak, James. Always have been. Always will be."

"You're not—"

"Would you mind just dropping me off? You've given me a lot to think about."

"Cher—"

"Please," she begs, breaking my heart.

"Sure. I'm not giving up. As long as you understand that."

She simply nods, slipping out the door without even a goodbye or a glance back.

Am I that easily forgotten? That easily left behind?

Or is this her pushing me away as hard as she can?

I won't let her give up on me so easily. There's nothing she can tell me that will dissuade me from grabbing my future—with her—by the horns and holding on tight.

CHAPTER 20

CAP

"HE'S IN JAIL." WEB'S TERSE VOICE COMES over the speaker in my car on my way to the gym. I figure I might as well get a workout in before heading to Rowdy's.

"For what?"

"Rape. Sexual assault. Robbery. Fraud. You name it, this guy's done it, according to his rap sheet. He's a dirty fuck."

"Where is he?" Hearing Cher's ex is locked up is good news. Not great—he could be dead, but behind bars will do.

"He's right there in Vegas, under Tumble Weed, if you can believe it."

"God, I haven't heard that name in a long time. The last time I saw him—"

"You were pulling his ass out of that burned-up shelter. He went stateside shortly after that," Web reminds me.

"Damn, that was a long time ago."

"Not long enough if you ask me." Web didn't leave the Marines on the best of terms. He got in trouble for his illegal gambling and ability to hack into any computer on base—or anywhere, for that matter. That's why he works for the CIA. He gets paid to do that shit now.

"You want me to reach out to Weed? Put a bug in his ear?"

It couldn't hurt. "Sure." It's not a bad idea to bring Tumble Weed, the warden, into the loop. Germain is locked up, but he's still bad news for the Stones he left behind.

"You got it. Hey, Cap?"

"Yeah?"

"You still got the burner?" He's referring to the burner phone so many of us have to communicate off the grid if need be.

"Affirmative." I'll always have one, just in case.

"Firm." He's willing to help if I need further assistance with Germain. I'm grateful but hope it won't be necessary.

"Semper Fi."

"Oorah."

The line disconnects. I continue to the gym, needing to hit something more than ever.

CHER

I can't avoid him forever. Maybe a week or two tops. Or so I thought. I made it a day. A whole friggin' day without feeling the need to reach out. Until...

"Mom, you there?"

"I'm here." Barely.

"You okay?"

Peachy. I could go my whole life and be perfectly fine never hearing my kids mention their dad again. I guess that's too much to ask. "Are you going to go?"

His sigh is long and muffled through the phone. "I don't know. I'll tell Ree today. See what she wants to do."

She won't want to go. I'm sure.

"Even if she doesn't go. I might. Not sure. But if she wants to go, then of course I'll be there. I'd never let her go alone."

Of course not. He's the best big brother. I couldn't ask for more from him. In fact, I've asked too much.

"You sure you're okay? You want me to come over once I'm done here?" His worry tugs at my heart.

"No. Go home to Frankie. I'm fine. Really." Total liar.

"Okay. I'll call you later."

"Gabriel, you focus on Frankie and my grandbaby. You don't need to fret over me any longer. Your father is in prison, dying. He can't hurt me, you, or Reese any longer."

He's not talking about the physical abuse. He's concerned with my mental status. After all, I was a shut-in for over three years. He just doesn't know it wasn't because of Germain.

"I'll *fret* over you if I want. It's my right. My duty," he insists.

"My sweet boy."

"Mom." He hates when I call him sweet. But he is. So, so very sweet to me.

"Go home, Gabriel. Give my love to Frankie and Maddox."

"Talk later."

He hangs up before I can reply or argue further. He'll do whatever he pleases, whatever eases his conscience and leaves room for what Frankie needs.

When there's a knock at the door, I realize I've been staring at the wall for nearly ten minutes. I'm not upset. I'm...

Another knock. Louder. It sounds peculiarly similar to James' knock, if that's even possible. Gah, how sad am I to tie a knock to the wish that it was James? I haven't talked to him since he dropped me off on Sunday afternoon. He's called and texted. I've ignored him, embarrassed and not sure where to go from where I left it.

The doorbell. Dang, okay. I'm coming.

"Cher, open the damn door. I'm not leaving. You can't ignore me."

Well, shit. I guess I do know his knock. Maybe not so silly after all.

With each twist of a lock, my anticipation grows. I've missed him. As much as I don't know what to do about that, one thing is clear. I like him. A lot.

Door open, I smile into his scowling face with green eyes that pierce my soul, make me feel less broken… Almost normal—or how I imagine a normal woman would feel about a guy she thinks entirely too much about.

"What part of 'don't leave me' do you not get?"

Thwap. That's the sound of his honesty hitting home.

"I didn't leave you. I've been right here." My voice is ridiculously wanton. I just want him to hold me. Not scold me. But I'm a little happy to see him upset again—at me. Or more specifically, elated to feel safe when he's upset and not fear it will escalate to abuse—his fist in my face.

"You've been ignoring me. It's the same, if not worse." There's sadness, hurt in his eyes.

Did I put that there? Does he consider me sneaking out and not returning his calls equal to Vera moving on—leaving him behind, so to speak? "You need time to heal."

His brows shoot up. "From what?"

"Losing Vera."

His sigh nearly blows me over. "I lost Vera over twenty years ago. I'm not mourning her."

I cross my arms. Waiting. Does he still love her? That's okay. She gave him two kids, and he just found out she'd dead. He has to be mourning the what-ifs even just a little bit. But if he's hung up on her, that's not okay. I don't want to complicate that by trying to start a relationship with him, personal or otherwise.

"Dammit, woman. I'm not pining over Vera. I made a lot of choices based on that heartbreak, but I'm not pining over her. I'm sad as fuck for Rowdy and Taylor losing their mom. I'm sad I missed out on raising them. But I don't hold any fairytales in my head that I would ever love Vera again—even if she wasn't dead."

It's my turn to frown. "You don't love her? She's not the reason you never got married, had kids?"

He holds up his hand, full of what looks to be bags of food. "Can I come in and we discuss this over lunch?"

"Sure." Not that discussing his ex is going to help my appetite. But I'll humor him. Hear him out.

In the kitchen, I scurry to clean up the mess of papers on the table. "What's all this?"

"Uh, nothing." I sweep the stacks together, making a huge mess of the details I've worked all morning on organizing. Well, I'll just have to do it again. It'll be a good exercise to see if I get the same outcome.

He scoffs. "It looks like the beginnings of a business plan to me, Cher. Does that mean you're considering my proposal?" He's so hopeful. He doesn't know what he's getting into.

"You shouldn't want me to. You're better off not tying yourself to me." I shrug, setting the folder full of papers aside. "But maybe I am." I can play coy if I want. I haven't decided. The details are a mess. He'll only think my ideas are silly.

I have no idea what I'm doing. I barely got my GED, and if it had been up to Germain, I never would have. He wanted me home, dependent, helpless, under his control at all times. Remaining uneducated and unable to drive only fed his need for control.

James captures my face in his palm, tipping my head back till our eyes meet. "He broke you good, didn't he?"

"Maybe a bit more than Vera did you." A lot more if I'm being honest. James can't possibly want me, and even if he did, he has to have lingering feelings for Vera to sort through. He never married, for god's sake. He's pining for her. Hoping she'd come back into his life. And she did, just not in the way he anticipated.

"I don't love her, Cher. I haven't for a long time. But I won't deny the affects her choices had on my life. Just like you can't deny the impact Germain has had on yours, even though he's been gone for nearly twelve years."

So he's not pining, regretting his missed opportunity to be with Vera?

I don't love Germain. I'm not sure I ever did. He was a means to escape my father. I couldn't see beyond that when I was fifteen. But Vera meant something different to James than Germain did to me. Good things.

He swipes at a tear I couldn't keep back. "When I think of her, all I remember is hurt and heartache. For Rowdy and Taylor's sake, I'm going to try to think of the good times, remember the good in her. But understand this: if she showed up today, begging me to take her back, I wouldn't. We could maybe be friends for the kids' sake, but I don't want her. *She's* not the one I'm set on." He leans down, face to face. "Do you understand me?"

"You don't love her."

"No."

"You're not pining over her."

He smirks. "No."

"You're focused on someone else."

"Bingo." He pulls out a kitchen chair and waits for me to sit. "Can you guess who that is?"

"Whoever she is, she's lucky." I'm not brave enough to say it's me. He needs to say it. I can barely hope it.

"Damn, are you that naive or just too stubborn to admit it?" He grazes my mouth with his.

My breath catches. This man, he's a walking, breathing example of seduction by honesty.

"It's you, Plum. It's fucking *you.*"

"Germain is in prison and dying," I blurt in a panic. James can't want me. He needs to know what he's getting—or more importantly, what he's not.

"Nope, he's not stealing this moment from us." James' mouth crashes over mine.

CHAPTER 21

CAP

CHRIST ALMIGHTY. THIS WOMAN AND HER irresistible mouth. I could kiss her for days, eat at her lips and tongue for eternity—and it would still never be enough. I squeeze her ass, grinding against her, and moan when she only tugs me closer.

I'm going to die from blue balls. I'm sure of it.

"Cher." I break our kiss and try to suck in air. "We have to stop." I don't want to, and it doesn't seem like she does either. But I refuse to be sideswiped by any triggers that might set her off. We need to talk. Figure out what she's comfortable with.

But first... "Be my girl."

She blinks at me as if I'm speaking in a foreign tongue.

"I want us to be on the same page—heading in the same direction." Not a fuck buddy. Never that. Not with her.

"And where's that?" The uncertainty in her tone reinforces my need to lay it all out for her.

"Forever, Cher. I want forever. I've known you longer than you've been without Germain." Granted I'd only met her once before Gabriel kicked out his deadbeat dad, but still, it's a long time. For a while I was only willing to be a protector, a confidant, nothing more.

By the time I realized I wanted more, I'd already ruined it by fucking around with my assistant. I didn't deserve Cher then, maybe not even now. "I want to try. What do you say?"

She stares at me for a long moment, frowns and steps out of my embrace and into the living room. I follow, not willing to let her out of my sight until I know where I stand. She stops in front of the picture window, turns, and wraps her arms around herself protectively. "I have scars."

I know. I've seen some. Felt the silvery pucker of others. "I don't care. You're beautiful."

Her frown deepens. "I've never had an orgasm." The shame in her words weighs down that statement, making it sad, not shameful.

"That's not a deterrent. It's an incentive." *Come on, what else you got, Cher? Give me your worst.* "You won't scare me off."

"Hmph." She shakes her head. "You've no idea."

"So, tell me." So I know and we can move past this.

"The more he hurt me, the more pain he caused, the more he enjoyed it." She defiantly crosses her arms, daring me to still want her.

Oh. Oh! Is... Does she have a kink thing? I'm not sure how I feel about that, but if that's what she needs, could I...? "Do... you get off on pain, Cher? Is that something you want or need?"

"No. God, no." She steps back, and her arms fall to her sides. She can't fathom how pain could be enjoyable.

My sigh of relief blows her hair back. "Good, 'cause I don't want to hurt you. I want to love you. But if you needed pain to feel pleasure, I'd get you there." I'd do anything to see her lax and satisfied in my arms, in my bed, in my heart. Always.

"I've never had sex for pleasure."

Jesus. All she's doing is making me want to hold her and love on her harder, deeper with a single-minded determination that'll have her coming until she begs me to stop. When I try to reply, she stops me with a glare.

Damn. My woman is hot when she finds her backbone.

"My father abused me. I thought Germain was saving me. Turns out it was more of the same. He saw weakness and ate me up like the big bad wolf."

Fuck. I'm going to kill that man. "Is your father alive?" If he is, I'm going to kill him too.

She smiles. "No. He attacked the wrong woman, got his throat cut."

Damn, she's happy about that. Good for her.

Also, hot as fuck.

She twists her lip and sits on the edge of the couch, her demeanor softening. We're getting to the heart of it. "Germain made Reese watch."

Jesus. In a beat of my heart, I've got her sequestered on my lap, in my arms. I'm going to rip that man limb from limb.

She sobs, "Gabriel doesn't know. B-but that's why Reese hates me. I wasn't strong enough. I should have left, no matter the consequences. I was weak, and my baby paid for it."

This right here is her kryptonite. Her shame is her undoing. Her memories, horrible and exploitative, drowning out her ability to truly move on.

"You were just a kid when you met Germain. How much older was he?"

"T-thirteen y-years," she answers through gut-wrenching sobs.

She was fifteen.

Kill. The. Motherfucker.

I tip her chin, garnering her eyes. "You were a victim of abuse from your father, then Germain, all while you were still a kid yourself. You were a kid raising kids. You didn't learn how to defend yourself. You didn't know how to get out. How to raise two kids on your own. He made sure you remained dependent on him. He wouldn't let you leave the house. You didn't get your GED until after he left. You had nothing. You'd left one abusive home only to find yourself in another. Sometimes the devil you know is better than the devil you don't. You can't punish yourself for not being able to get out sooner. What happened to Gabriel and Reese at the hands of Germain are on him, not you—not solely. When you're ready? You talk to them. I doubt they'd want you carrying this shame—guilt. I don't believe they blame you. They blame him. You were a victim too."

Her whole life she's been abused by two men who should have represented safety. She doesn't know what that even means.

"I'm never going to harm you, Cher. I'm never going to blame you for what happened. And I'm sure as hell not walking out that door because of the crimes done *to* you and your kids. It sucks for you all, but your kids have found ways to move on. You need to too." I kiss her forehead. "Let me help. Let me be your safe place to land. Let me be your rock, your cheerleader, your protector. I need you, Cher. Please, need me."

Her sobs continue, but her holding me tight and secure gives me hope. One cry, one awful confession is not enough, but it's a start.

My woman thinks she's weak. She's a fucking warrior.

CHAPTER 22

CAP

I BLEW OFF MY DAY. THERE WAS NO WAY I WAS leaving Cher after all her confessions, trying to scare me off. I may never leave, just to prove to my stubborn minx I'm not running because of her past.

Lying on her bed, holding her as she sleeps, I doze on and off, waking every time she moves or makes a sound.

I'm rock hard, despite telling my body to ignore the sleeping beauty in my arms. She rolls half on me, nuzzling my neck, and her hand lands on my pec, her leg, over mine, inches ever higher as she undulates her hips, rubbing herself against me.

Christ Almighty, even in sleep she's a siren.

"James," she whispers. When her mouth skims across my neck and latches on with the tiniest chuckle, I know she's awake and teasing the beast.

"Cher," rumbles from deep in my chest.

She fucking moans, her hips press harder, and her fingers dig into my flesh.

Never had an orgasm. Unfathomable. The woman working herself up in my arms is not the same one who's never shot off like a rocket. This one knows exactly what she wants and where she needs it.

I roll over, pinning her beneath me. "What's on your mind, Plum?" Before she can answer, I swallow her gasps with my mouth, delving in when she opens, offering her tongue in thanks. I grind against her sweet pussy, drawing more moans and gasps.

Perfection. Sheer. Utter. Perfection.

When she wraps her legs around my hips, I know it's time to cool the jets. With great reluctance, I release her mouth, drop my head to her shoulder, catch my breath, and gain control of my need to pound her into tomorrow.

"I don't want to hurt you," I mumble into her neck before I push up, hovering over her, braced on my arms. "Tell me what's okay and what's not."

The flush of her skin catches my attention before I remember why I'm not kissing her stupid.

She tugs at my shirt. "I want you, James."

One quick kiss for the sexy-as-fuck way my name sounds coming out of her mouth.

"I need you," she breathes against my lips. "Show me how it can be."

I study her puffy, tired eyes from crying, not sure I could ever say no to an offer like that, but I need to be sure. "Tell me exactly what you're asking for."

When all I get is her deer in the headlights look, I nuzzle her nose with mine and help her find her brave. "Are you just wanting me to love on you and make you come?" I kiss her mouth, not missing the hope shining in her eyes. "Or are you wanting my cock inside you?"

Damn, that blush of hers is everything. "Yes, to both."

That's my brave warrior. "You change your mind at any time, you tell me. You don't like something, you tell me. Understand?"

"Yep." She nods, biting her lips, turning my insides over. She fists my hair before our lips connect. "And if I like something?"

My smile breaks free, so damn happy she's already thinking she'll like what I plan to do to her. "Your body will tell me, Cher. But if you want to add your words, you go right ahead." I drop a kiss to the corner of her mouth. "Tell me every delicious"—kiss to the other corner—"dirty little thing you like. In detail," I add as I dive in, taking no prisoners, just deep soul-sucking kisses that leave me ready to pound and her begging to come.

When I'm sure she can't take much more, and she's not changing her mind—not that she still can't, I pull off my shirt and undo my jeans, giving me room to breathe. I slip off her shorts without any problem, but when I go for her shirt, she grips my wrist, fear lacing her features. "You're beautiful, Cher. Let me prove it."

I reward her trust when she releases me with a lingering kiss, then slip her shirt off and still. "Damn, baby." I suck in air at the sight of her tight little body, high breasts, flat stomach, and smoking hot deep purple bra and panties.

Does she always wear this hot shit under her clothes? I'm going to have to check it out every damn time now that she's my woman.

She fidgets. I've stared too long, and she doesn't get why. I still her hands moving to cover herself. "There are no words, Cher." I'm getting fucking choked up. She's ashamed of her scars, but I've barely even noticed. It breaks my heart she doesn't know what a smoking hot, perfectly put together woman she is.

I begin a slow crawling gaze up her body again.

"James," she cries, eyes watering.

"No. Fuck." I'm screwing this up. "You take my breath away, Cher. You're so fucking beautiful it hurts. Swear. I'm in awe, baby."

She palms my cheek. "You were staring. It's not bad? You're not lying?" A tear slips free.

"A Monet is still a Monet even if it's sliced in half." I lay a kiss right between the swells of her breasts I'm dying to get a hold of. "Be mine, Cher. Say it, please."

Fuck, I'm ready to beg.

"Yes," she breathes, her eyes fluttering shut, only to open again, pleading.

"Not just sex. Everything. Dating. A relationship. I want it all, Plum."

Her back arches as if I just slipped inside her. "Yes," she moans.

I'm done. Never been this hard. Never this desperate to make a woman come.

A flew flicks of my wrist and her panties are gone and her bra lies on the floor next to them. Her rosy nipples top her plump breasts as I squeeze and knead, running my tongue along each crest and valley before sucking each deeply and not too gently.

My girl not only takes it, she begs for more, her hands holding me to her, pulling as she arches into my mouth. She's a fucking dream.

"Cher," I rasp, needing inside her.

Her hips rise and fall, seeking, needing to be touched, kissed, sucked, and fucked.

I traverse her body, exploring with my hands and mouth, slipping lower and lower. She gasps and scrapes my scalp with her nails when I reach her patch of perfectly manicured dark curls, slipping my tongue between her folds and groaning my satisfaction at finding her so perfectly wet and pungently sweet.

Christ. I could live here.

And I do for the next few minutes, for that's all it takes for my warrior to find her battle cry and fall apart for me.

So fucking sexy.

So fucking mine.

I don't stop. I lick and suck her clit until she's begging me to stop. Until she's writhing and pleading to come again.

And damn if she doesn't.

My broken woman comes like she was made to be mine, waiting on me to feast on her, every delicious, perfect, scarred, gorgeous inch of her. All mine.

CHAPTER 23

CHER

WHEN THE FIRST ORGASM HIT ME, I HONESTLY feared for my next breath. Nothing I'd read prepared me for *that*. I wasn't sure if I'd survive it or catch a full breath again. Entirely too turned on to be embarrassed, I spread my legs wider, gripped his hair, and begged with every fiber of my body for him to do it again.

He did.

Again.

And again.

Three heart-stopping, breathtaking orgasms later, I still want him. I *need* him.

"Please, James," I plead for him to fill me.

He rears back, his face glistening with my pleasure. *My pleasure.* Ohmygod! I never thought… I never wanted until him. Now. Now, I can't imagine going a second without him inside me, without him loving me.

A full body shiver runs its course as he tugs off his jeans and boxer briefs. His impressive length bobs on his equally impressive six-pack. Damn, I've never seen a body so fit and so made for fucking.

Eagerly, I spread my legs, my hips flexing, needing him, goosebumps rippling along my skin at his heated gaze locked on my core, licking my taste off his lips.

"Dammit, Cher, your hunger is about to end me."

"Then hurry up and fill me. I need you." It's so far beyond want. He's my drug, and I need my fix.

He kneels on the bed, hovering over me. "I need to be in charge—on top, Cher. Are you okay with that?"

God, yes. I whimper and nod quickly. I need him to take the lead.

His hard cock settles against me when he lowers himself between my legs. I flex, trying to get him where I need him. He slips so easily between my lady lips, drenched with desire.

"Cher," he warns, then exhales deeply, "Fuck, I don't have a condom. I didn't plan—" Regret furrows his brow.

I can't— "I won't get pregnant. I haven't been with anyone since Germain, and thankfully disease-free."

"Same. I haven't been with anyone in a long time. And not without a condom since Vera." He winces. "Sorry to bring her up."

"It's fine. You don't have to filter your thoughts about her. She was a huge, impactful part of your life. I don't begrudge you or want you to hide any part of that from me."

"Okay." He flexes, his cock slipping closer to my entrance. "You sure? We could do other stuff?"

"Don't you dare stop."

He chuckles and kisses along my jaw. "Not stopping, Plum. I just want to be sure you're alright."

"I won't be until you're inside me."

"Damn, woman, love your spunk." He grips my leg behind the knee and lifts. "Hold on." He brings our mouths together, whispering, "Gonna love you now, Cher."

Yes, is all I can think when he fills me in one long, slow thrust. I grip his shoulders, holding on, arching, clutching, shuddering with every in and out movement.

Deliciously slow, deep, and grinding, he enters me only to pull out and do it again.

And again.

I wrap my legs around him, and he sinks deeper still. I want to swallow him whole, never let him go. I had no idea sex could feel like this.

"Jesus, Plum. You feel so fucking good."

Yes. Yes. So. So good. I brace my hand on the headboard, trying to ground myself to push back, rising to meet him. "Ohmygod."

"That's it, baby. Feel me deep. So fucking deep."

Oh, yes!

Yes!

Ohmygod. Ohmygod. Ohmygod.

"Fuck," he groans, thrusting harder.

"Yes!" I… he… Ohmygod!

The ringing starts in my ears as the frisson of pleasure starts in my toes, tingling, building, growing, and sliding up my body. "I…"

"Goddamn, baby," he growls as I come, shaking, gripping him so tight.

Please, God, don't let me die, I beg as I fill and fill and fill and then burst into a million shards of my former self. I don't even care if I can be put back together.

Then slowly, I do.

His lips. His hands. His cock all bring me back to life and build and build and ohmyfuckinggod I'm coming again.

"Fuck. Fuck. Fuck." Hot jolts fill me, and he groans, squeezing me so, so tight, holding me together as I quake and pray to never, never, never lose this man.

Please, God.

Please.

Please.

CAP

I fall to the mattress, trying to catch my breath and make sense of what the hell just happened. She came like five times. Three on my tongue. Two on my cock. Not that I'm counting. Alright, I'm counting, but not for my ego, but for her well-being. She... "You alright, Cher?"

She blinks up at me, sweat glistening on her silky soft skin, and nods.

"Words, baby. I need to hear you tell me you're okay." Please, *please* be alright.

A smile tips her lips. "Never, and I truly mean, *never* better."

"That's good. That's real good. Cause I plan on doing that a lot." Like in fifteen minutes, a lot.

"Like the rest of the day?"

Damn. "The rest of my life."

Her brows jump, then settle. "In different places? Different positions?"

I'm kinda partial to the one we just did. "If that's what you want."

She shrugs, and I haul her ass on top of me, capturing her eyes. "You tell me what you want, and it's yours, Plum."

"I'll make a list."

I nearly choke on my tongue laughing. "Who are you? And where's my reticent, 'broken' girl?"

She preens. "For the first time in my life, I don't feel broken."

My heart picks up, and my cock stirs. "Because you're not, Cher. You're perfect."

Ten minutes later...

"Fuck, baby." I'm riding her from behind, gripping her hips like handles, slamming into her, drilling for that sweet spot that's gonna make her ignite and squeeze me so good.

"Ohmygod," she purrs on repeat with each thrust. "I'm..." Her words morph into a scream. Her body seizes and shakes. Her arms give out, and she falls face down on the bed, her ass still up in the air only because of my hold on her.

I grind my pleasure into the vise grip she has on my cock, coming hard enough to lose sight for a few seconds.

Still buried deep, I wrap my hand around her waist and roll to my side, spooning her from behind, slowly sliding in and out of her, not yet spent. She contracts around me every few seconds as her whole body jolts with echoes of her orgasm.

My brave girl guides my hand between her legs, letting me know she's not done.

With shallow thrusts, my fingers rub her swollen clit. I lick and suck on her neck and shoulder, whispering dirty deeds and sweet temptations into her ear, mumbling, "Pinch your nipples."

Moaning, she does just that, the sight getting me rock hard again. I'm like a teenager. Can't stop coming. Can't stop getting hard.

Wave after wave of full body thrusts, and she's completely wrapped in my arms, my mouth pressed to her ear. "Gonna fuck you all night, Cher. All morning, and into the next day. Gonna fill you so good and full, you'll never forget you're mine."

"Ohmygod, James," she coos, gripping my arms. Her sweet pussy clenches, milking, begging for my cum.

I pinch her clit, rubbing harder, thrusting deeper, hitting her G-spot from behind, wishing for the first time in my life I had my cock pierced for her pleasure.

"Yes, ohmygod, yes."

On the verge of losing my mind, ready to beg her to come so I can fill her full, she lets loose, hits the turbo button and ignites like a rocket, taking me with her with each squeeze of her pussy and cry of my name.

CHAPTER 24

CHER

I AGREED TO LET JAMES HELP ME WITH THE bakery, but I want a partnership, both inside the bakery and out. He can be as involved as he wants. The kitchen is mine, but the business side, he's taking lead—thank God, considering I have no idea. But I want to learn. He promises to show me the ropes, not taking a dime until the business is in the black for a solid year or more. He's also looking for a manager to help me run the place so I can focus on baking, and he can't be there every day, given he has his own business to run.

It's a gift. A big fat gift. And I'm taking it.

He agreed to keep it a secret for now. Reese is finding her footing with Rowdy, who has a big fight coming up. Gabriel has Frankie and Ox to worry over. Plus, the whole Germain dying and wanting to see them one last time thing. They don't need to fret over me.

Germain's lawyer called, advising he wanted to see me too. I told him *no*. There's no way I'm stepping foot in that prison or within spitting distance of that man. Dying or not, I don't want to set eyes on him again.

He can't die soon enough for me. He can go to hell and keep my father company. Maybe they can take turns raping each other. That sounds fitting and like the justice neither of them saw in life.

It's mid-week, a few days since I also agreed to be James' girlfriend, and we had sex. I mean, mind-bending, earthquake-rocking sex. He's insatiable—or maybe I am. Does it matter? All that really matters is I'm not broken. I'm not an icy bitch—at least not with *him*. I feel as young as ever, and James makes me feel desired, beautiful, and perfect just as I am—scars and all.

I had no idea being so *seen* would be so freeing.

And such a turn on.

I squirm in my seat. *Focus.*

I'm working on the menu. I'm going to keep it simple with key items, then slowly incorporate new recipes. I thought it might be cool to have a tasting day where customers taste a new recipe and vote on whether to add it to the menu or not. I'll also have holiday or seasonal treats that will rotate throughout the year.

Walker, one of Cap's fighters and a computer whiz—who knew?—is working on a phone app for location details, menu, ordering, voting on new items, and a rewards program. He'll also install my POS software, linking it to the app, and show me how to use it. All of this is under the radar since it's a secret.

My phone rings, and James' name pops on the screen. I school my silly heart for beating faster. What this man does to me shouldn't be this amazing and life-altering.

"I ordered your sign," he says before I can even say hello.

"Hi."

"Fuck. Sorry. Hi, Plum. I ordered your sign." He rushes on, so happy I went with his suggestion of *Sugarplum's*. I didn't have a better idea, and I liked naming my bakery for a nickname he calls me. It's sweet. And if you can't have something sweet regarding a bakery, then when can you?

"I guess this is really happening, then?"

"Well, if it doesn't, we can always put it over my bed."

"Does that mean *you're* Sugarplum's?" I'm teasing, but want to see what he says. I'm always testing the waters, pushing a little further, feeling him out.

"Did I not make that clear, Cher? I'm two hundred percent yours."

Be still my heart.

When I don't respond because I have no idea how to do this, how to flirt, he says, "You still there? Does that scare you?"

"To pieces," I admit.

"Cher, I got you. I promise."

Tears threaten. I fight through the tightness in my throat. "Don't be nice to me."

"Damn, baby, all I want to do is be nice to you… dirty… and sweet."

"That sounds like a new dessert: Dirty and Sweet." I swipe my eyes as the idea for a new dessert comes to mind. I make a note. I'll have to play around with the recipe later, but what a great idea to give desserts playful names on the menu, not just what they actually are.

"Can I be your taste tester?"

"Absolutely." That sounds like fun. Fun. Who knew a relationship could be *fun*?

"Don't forget our appointment later to meet with the appliance guy and the contractor. You pick what you want, and they'll make sure it fits."

"Okay." The cost scares me. Tom gave me a significant boost to what I had saved, but, either way, James doesn't want me to use it. I can't argue with his justification of fronting the money and saving the cash for a rainy day. A buttload of cash sitting in a high-yield savings account, that will be moved to a money market account as soon as we have that appointment next week. Investing. I never thought I'd have the funds to do that.

"You got this, Plum. I have faith in you and your vision, and your amazing touch in the kitchen. Everything you make is perfection. The bakery will be no different."

"Thank you... for everything."

"The only thanks I want is free sweets."

"All you can eat, Cap."

"Damn, I love you calling me James, but when you say Cap, it does something to me. Like you're finally admitting you're mine. You are, aren't you, Cher? All mine?"

My breath hitches, and goosebumps break out. "I want to be. I want to be your Belle."

"You are. You soothe my beast, cut the barbwire from around my heart, Cher. You do that. No one else."

"When are you coming home?"

He laughs. It's deep and full and does crazy things to my insides. "Not soon enough." There's talking in the background. "I gotta go. I'll see you this afternoon for that meeting."

"See ya, Cap."

"Damn. Love that."

Love you... I bite my tongue. I can't be the one to say it first. It's too soon anyway. It's all the sex clouding my brain, teasing my heart into thinking it's love and not desire.

CAP

I seek out Rowdy on my way to meet Cher. I find him lifting weights with Cowboy and Jess. Rowdy is pushing hard, getting ready for his fight. Since making my big announcement about him being my son by blood, I've tried to give him space, not distract him from his fight. He's got enough going on with Reese and her father.

When I step in, Cowboy and Jess give me space with quick *hey, Cap* greetings, then move to the other side of the room.

"Cap." Rowdy gives me a chin nod and takes a drink.

"How's it going?" Things could be really awkward between us, but we didn't miss a beat. I always felt a connection to him, now it just feels deeper, justified in some way. The guys have been cool. No grumbling. No contention about favoritism. We're a close-knit family, blood or not. The news of Rowdy's lineage didn't sidetrack that at all. I'm proud of my guys for being stand-up men. Ones I admire and am proud to back, in and out of the ring.

"Good. Trying to stay focused."

"You do what you need to do. I got your back." He loves Reese, that much is clear. If he needs her—or she needs him to be there for her in a more substantial way, I'm not going to balk about it. I get it. The closer I get to Cher, the more I understand the intense love I've seen between Gabriel and Frankie, and now Rowdy and Reese.

"I appreciate that." He leans in close. "Gabriel told me about you and..." He glances to the guys ignoring us. But he doesn't say her name. I appreciate his discretion.

"Do we need to talk about it?" I didn't even consider he might have feelings about it beyond Cher being Reese's mom. I was once in love with *his* mom, after all.

"No. I mean, if you want to, but not because I have any problem with it."

"Good. She's a little skittish about it, wanting to keep it under wraps for a while longer."

"Not a problem. I talked to Taylor today. She's asking lots of questions about Barrett and me. Why we're hardly talking. I have a feeling she's going to find out soon. Are you okay with that?"

"Fuck, yes. I want her to know. I'd like a chance to get to know her too. Be... *whatever* she wants me to be in her life. I've missed so much already."

His smile is huge, the dimples we share popping out. "You'll love her. She's a trip."

"I've no doubt."

He tosses his bottle in the recycle bin. "I gotta wrap this. I'm picking up dinner tonight."

So domestic. "Knock it out." We fist bump.

I wave goodbye to Cowboy and Jess and head out to meet my woman, nailing down more details of the bakery. Then if I'm lucky, nailing her.

CHAPTER 25

CHER

I'M AN EARLY RISER, ALWAYS HAVE BEEN. AS A KID, it was a means to escape the house before anyone woke up, and I got in trouble or worse. With Germain, it was a means to prepare for whatever his mood brought and, of course, the kids. After Germain, I was up way before the sun to bake, to make the best living I could without working outside the house.

Even though I don't have to, at the moment, I still wake up early. It's a habit I've no intention of breaking. The bakery will be ready in a month or so and will require early hours again. Being ready to open depends a lot on finishing the construction for the whole shopping center and parking lot, plus the buildout of the individual storefronts. Physically, the bakery could be ready in a few weeks, but we have staff to hire, train, and need to test out recipes in the commercial kitchen. I'm a home baker, not professionally trained, completely self-taught from cookbooks, then the internet, and my imagination. Trial and error have always been my way. I don't envision that changing.

Cinnamon rolls cool on the stove as I sip my morning coffee on Cap's porch swing, enjoying the cooler temperatures and gentle breeze, wrapped in a blanket. I heard the shower turn on when I stepped outside. I imagine Cap will be down soon. He had a late night with Rowdy's fight that he won. I couldn't bring myself to go, though I know I should have been there to support him. Too many people. Instead, I sat in Cap's home waiting on him and fretting over Gabriel and Reese's visit with Germain.

They didn't call last night. I'm hoping that's a good sign. But one never knows. I should have called them, but I was afraid of what they'd say, afraid to open that can of worms. Though I suppose it's already been open for a while now—rotting up the place.

"Plum." Cap steps out the back door, handing me his phone. "Gabriel has been trying to reach you."

"Oh, I… Where is my phone?" Maybe still charging or in my purse. I'm not tied to it like so many. I so rarely use it. I suppose that will have to change with the business.

"Cher?" Cap sits next to me, still holding the phone out, swapping it for my cup of coffee he takes a large gulp from.

"Sorry." Jeez, scatterbrained much? "Hello?"

"Mom." Gabriel sounds tired, his voice rough from sleep.

"Good morning." I fight to sound chipper when all I feel is dread.

"Do you remember the Fourth of July before I kicked Dad out?"

"I, um…" Twelve years ago? I barely remember what I ate yesterday. "Why are you asking?" I flash to Cap, his concerned gaze already on me.

"I just need you to think. Is there anything you can remember about that Fourth? It was only a few weeks before Dad got the boot. It's important, Mom."

Clearly. "Give me a second." I usually baked on the Fourth for the neighborhood fair and fireworks. "I think you and Reese went to watch the fireworks with some friends. Your father was drunk—not unusual."

"Wait. I remember. Ree and I went with… Gah, I can't remember his name. But… We spent the night at his house because we didn't want to come home knowing Dad was drunk."

He wasn't always, but he was drunk often enough, and that only made him worse. He was mean sober. He was *evil* drunk.

"Lola came over looking for you. She stayed the night, but I told her to stay in Reese's room. Out of sight from Germain."

"*Lola* was in Ree's bed?" He sounds sick about it.

"What's this about, Gabriel? What happened with your father?"

"Did you know he used to come in Ree's room at night? Touch himself. Make her watch?"

"What?!" I thought I'd spared her. Had that bastard done worse when I wasn't there? When he was alone with her? I'm on my feet, running for the lawn before I puke all over Cap. I only make it down the stairs and a few feet before a large arm wraps around my waist.

"Shhh, Cher. I got you," Cap whispers in my ear, holding me to his chest.

I crumble, taking us both to the grass. "No, no, no," I cry.

Cap takes his phone I managed to hold on to. "Gabriel, your mom's a wreck. What did you say?"

I can't hear his words, but I hear the gruff of my son's voice, and the rumble in Cap's chest as he tenses around me. "Christ." The agony on his face matches that in my heart.

My girl. My sweet girl. What have I done?

"I'm putting you on speaker." Cap holds the phone between us.

"What else did he do, Mom? When I wasn't there?" Gabriel asks, pain and anger evident in each word.

"H-he used to make…" I can't. I can't say those words to my son. I silently beg Cap to make this go away.

"Can I tell him?" Cap asks.

I nod, when all I really want to do is run far away and die a quick and painless death. No. What I really want to do is kill Germain slowly and painfully.

"Gabriel, son." Cap pulls me tighter. For his comfort, for mine, or maybe to be sure I actually don't run off. "Germain would rape your mother in front of Reese. Make her watch."

No. No. No. No… I melt into Cap's increasingly tighter embrace, hiding my face, dying inside from shame that I couldn't be strong enough to stop it. The words too much to hear coming from his mouth to Gabriel's ears.

"Jesus fucking Christ. That sonofabitch, I'm going to kill him," Gabriel seethes.

"Get in line, son."

If only he would.

"Mom, I'm so sorry. I'm sorry I wasn't there," my son tries to blame himself.

I sit up, wipe my face and grip Cap's hand around the phone. "Gabriel, you listen to me. None of this is your fault. You were just a kid. You deserved to live the life of a kid, not a watchdog. You saved us so many times, you have no idea, and in the end, you did what I couldn't. You kicked him out. You are not to blame here."

"You sure as fuck are not to blame here either." His anger is palpable. "You feel me, Mom? You are *not* to blame."

He's wrong. It's my fault. All of it. If I'd never—

"Dad said he raped Reese on the Fourth of July. That's why I was asking."

"No! Oh, Jesus!" My stomach rolls, threatening to discard my morning coffee.

"Mom. Mom! It wasn't Reese. It was Lola. It wasn't Reese, Mom." He keeps talking. His words buzz in my ears, but it doesn't make it better.

It doesn't make it better that he raped someone else that night. It matters that Germain thought he could get away with it at all.

And, until now, he has.

I'm finally strong enough.

"I'm going to kill him." I stand, collecting myself. A calm seeps through my veins. "He's dead."

I need my phone. I'll call his lawyer and get a visit arranged. Then I'll kill him with my bare hands if need be. I'll peel his skin off one layer at a time. Slowly and very, very painfully.

CHAPTER 26

CAP

I T'S BEEN A FEW WEEKS SINCE THE GERMAIN NEWS blew up Cher's family—my family. She's in my bed or me hers every night. We're more than dating. We're practically living together. Fuck, I want that. I want her here in my house, permanently.

I've tried to take it slow, give her space to get her sea legs or her Cap legs, whatever. But it's getting harder to keep our relationship a secret— well, a secret from everyone except Gabriel, Rowdy, Walker, and basically anyone involved with the bakery, which is also a secret from her family— my family.

Too many damn secrets.

And my woman has her own secret she's keeping from me and everyone else. Everyone. She's made arrangements to see Germain. The man she swore she'd never want to lay eyes on again. She's purposely going to see him. If she thinks she's going alone, she's got another thing coming.

And if she thinks she's going to kill him… Yeah, well, that's not happening either. He's not taking the rest of her life away when she goes to prison for killing a man who deserved to die a long time ago—like in the womb.

Not happening on my watch.

She's been eerily calm since Gabriel and Reese visited their father, the news that Germain used to masturbate and make Reese watch, that he raped Lola believing it was Reese. Sick fucker.

He needs to die. I agree, but not by Cher's hands. Her strength is astounding, but I'm not sure she can withstand the guilt of taking another life, even if it's Germain's.

"You ready?" She steps into the kitchen, hot as hell in her flowy blue dress and sandals. Her chest and upper arms are covered. Only a few scars show on her forearms, small, white, barely noticeable. I have to search to even notice them now. But she rarely wears anything that shows her back or upper torso. Legs, though, she'll show for days, and they're quite beautifully showing through the side slits as she walks.

I harden at the idea of touching her, getting her off before we leave. "Cher."

She whips her head around, my want evident in my tone. Her gaze locks with mine before traveling lower. My cock lengthens at her perusal. "What's on your mind, Cap?"

Fuck. She had to go and call me *Cap*. "Cher. Here. Now."

She floats toward me. I'm not even sure her feet move. She's a goddess, tempting me, making me reckless, making us late. I'm never late. I hate to be late except when it comes to loving my woman.

"Hands on the counter, Plum."

Want courses through me when she shivers at my command. Hands on the counter, she throws a lustful look over her shoulder, biting her lip, flexing her hips. I sweep her hair to one side, nibble on the skin below her ear, whispering, "You want me, baby?"

Her back arches in another shudder.

"Fuck. So responsive." My hands slip up her outer thighs, gathering the material, pulling the dress up around her waist. I bite her shoulder. "Tell me."

"I want you, please."

"That's my girl." I grind my erection against her, but she's too short for me to enter her standing up. I need her higher, or I'll bust a knee ligament trying to squat and fuck at the same time. "Hold on."

I lift her, walk around the island to the high stools on the other side, pull a seat out and set her down facing the high bar away from me. "Pull your dress up, Plum. Hold it around your waist." I unzip and breathe a sigh of relief when my cock hits the air. Hard as stone for her. Always. Like a teen all over again.

I pat her bitable ass. "Scoot back, ass hanging off."

"James?" The worry in her tone gives me pause.

I kiss her shoulder and tip her chin to me. "No ass play, Cher. Just better access." Relief floods her face. "You still good?"

She tugs me down and devours my mouth, telling me with her tongue and mouth just how good she is. I slide my hand down her backside, pulling her thong to the side and slip my fingers through her wetness. She sucks my tongue hard when I slip a finger inside.

So fucking mine.

Positioned behind her, I tease her entrance with my cock. She leans forward, her ass falling back more, and I slip inside. I want to slap her ass for rushing me, but— "Fuck." I thrust in all the way, relish her gasp, and nearly come from the wet heat kissing all along my cock. "Mine, Cher. So. Fucking. Mine," I grit, thrusting through each word.

"Cap."

"Fuck, that's right. Say my name, Plum. Don't stop." I wrap around her, one arm banding her chest and palming a breast so firm and full, the nipple deliciously pokes my hand. "I want to suck your nips till you come, Cher."

Fuck! She clenches and moans.

My woman loves my dirty mouth—on her or spouting all the ways I want to make her come. And damn if it doesn't get me harder, voracious with want and the need to fill her with my cock and my cum.

My other arm around her waist, I finger her clit. "So fucking wet, Cher. You're gonna have our juices dripping down your thighs all day, aren't you, baby?"

"Yes. Ohmygod, yes!"

"You're gonna smell like me." Hard thrust. "You're gonna feel me all fucking day, Cher." Thrust. Thrust. Thrust. "You gonna contract around nothing, wishing my cock was still inside you." Deep grind.

"Yes!"

I piston in and out. Fucking close. "You're gonna want to finger yourself to ease the ache. But you won't. 'Cause you know only my cock can get you there."

"Ohmygod, Cap. Ohmygod. Ohmy…" She cries, locking up, wrapping around my arms, pussy walls squeezing my cock, begging for my seed, she comes in a gush of heat that has my eyes rolling into the back of my head.

I come so fucking hard, I grasp the counter to stop from falling over. Leaning into her, I pump and pump until she's so full, it's dripping out, and I've got nothing left to give but my heart.

Take it, Cher. It's all yours. I think it has been for a long time now. Maybe from the first time I tasted your plum tarts and chocolate cake all those years ago.

Holding her tight, I kiss along her shoulder. "You alright, Sugarplum?"

She gulps in a big breath and lets it out slowly, her weight fully in my arms. "Better than. I'm perfect."

Damn straight. So fucking perfect.

CHAPTER 27

CHER

I FEEL HIM EVERYWHERE. THE TIPS OF HIS FINGERS, the flat of his palm, the warmth of his mouth, the driving force of his cock. He's everywhere. I turn around and come face to face with his scent trailing behind me, and for a split second I think he really is here. Then I blush and giggle like a schoolgirl with a crush, a secret, a hidden desire.

That is my day, giving me pause, giving me thrills, and keeping me wet in anticipation of being the recipient of his burning hot affection again and again.

He consumes me.

He obliterates me.

He shatters me and puts me back together better than I was to begin with.

The future he shows me shines so bright, it frightens and thrills me in equal measure. Almost like pain and pleasure. *It hurts so good.* A sentiment I now understand.

Everything is so good. Too good. The walk-through is finished. The bakery is nearly ready to open in a few weeks. The staff starts on Monday, training, working out routines, recipes, procedures, getting the feel for the place and each other. Then we'll have a soft opening, taste tests, and open house, before officially opening our doors when the entire complex is complete. A grand opening. It's thrilling.

But for now, I'm making lists, waiting on the delivery of the office furniture and tables and chairs for out front. The patio furniture comes next week. Everything else is here, installed, ready to go.

Tomorrow I start baking, getting to know my new equipment. There are no deliveries, no appointments. Just me and my new kitchen to christen. I can't wait.

My gaze falls to the front of the shop through the window in the wall that divides the front of the shop where customers will dwell and the back of the shop where the magic will happen. My kitchen. *My* bakery.

Take that, Germain.

Your terror didn't ruin me for life. Your scars may reside on my body, but they don't rule me. You and your hateful ways don't control me anymore. And if I have my way, you won't be tainting this world with your presence much longer. You will draw your last breath, and I will be there to see it slip from your body and the evil die in your eyes as you leave this life to dwell forever in hell.

I may join you one day for taking your life, but it will be worth it. And until then, I'm going to earn our kids' love, love Cap hard, live without regret, and take each day as a gift without you in it.

The beep of the back door startles me. We just had the alarm system installed. It's set to beep every time the back door opens. It might just irritate the hell out of me, but for now it stays on. I can always mute it later.

A few seconds before I hear footfall, I glance at the security monitor above my head, expecting to see a delivery truck out back. There's none. It's an empty parking lot and a construction dumpster.

Before I can fully turn toward the back hallway, a meaty hand seizes my neck.

"Mrs. Stone, I've been dying to meet you." He squeezes, cutting off my air. "Germain sends his love."

CAP

My cock has a mind of its own. He's usually so well behaved, too. Every time Cher pops into my head, my cock stirs, begging for his woman again. I don't blame him. She's hot as fuck and so damn responsive. For a woman who's never had enjoyable sex in her life—don't get me hating—she's my fucking dream. My ideal.

I'm ashamed at how long it took me to figure out my shit. Vera did a number on me, but I was only a kid, barely eighteen when I left her—not counting the two hot and heavy episodes that ended up impregnating her. *I* left *her*. Her response in return hurt me more, but I started it. I wasn't man enough to stay. I wasn't man enough to come back and take what I felt was mine. And sadly, I wasn't man enough to truly let her go and move the fuck on.

The love I held for her died. I'm not even sure when. I'm not even sure it *was* love and not ego and want. The latter, I only discovered when I realized how I felt for Vera was nothing compared to how I feel for Cher. It doesn't even compare, compute, or exist on the same plane. My love and need for Cher are in the stratosphere. My feelings for Vera were more ground level, hormonal pubescent puppy love, mixed with brotherly rivalry and a shit ton of ego.

I'm a fucking idiot. All these years wasted. Broken and angry. For what? Puppy love?

I make my way through the gym, finding Rowdy and Gabriel sparring. Since Rowdy's fight, they've become sparring partners. No one else is brave enough to take either of them on when they go full nuclear, with Jonah riding their asses to *take it easy*.

Man, what a match it would be to see these two go at it in the ring during an official match. Not just for the money, but the pure enjoyment of the sport and watching gods in action. I'm not even sure who'd win. A year ago, I would have said Gabriel, hands down. But Rowdy's found his fire, and it's attached to Reese. I'm not sure he'd let himself go full dark on Gabriel for Reese's sake. But man, I'd love to see it as long as I knew they'd come out of it in one piece and still as close as they are now.

With that thought, I shake off the idea. Their friendship—their bond—is more important than the outcome of a paid fight. This, right here, is what they love. The pure adrenaline of combat, mano a mano, brother to brother... Loyal, brave and true, like Gabriel's tattoo.

Rowdy catches my gaze over Gabriel's shoulder. He holds up his hand, chinning toward me. Gabriel turns, his ferocity turning into concern. Rowdy mumbles something to Jonah, and they both jump the ropes, grabbing their shit and heading to me.

Am I doing this? *Fuck*. I head out back, not a word spoken. They follow. Their heavy breathing leads their near silent steps, graceful and stealthy fucks.

Agitation and uncharted territory have me on edge.

"What is it, Cap?" Gabriel breaches the silence and my deafening thoughts.

I stop at the edge of the lake, wishing I'd put in some benches, picnic tables, or left some folding chairs—something—out here.

"Is it Cheryl?" Rowdy adds, moving closer, swiping at the sweat on his face and chest, pulling on a t-shirt and shoes. Gabriel does the same.

I eye them both. This is not normal guy shit. Do they want to know? Do I owe them an explanation?

"Whatever it is, just spit it out. Let us help." Gabriel, ever the healer, the caretaker.

I take few breaths and lock on Rowdy. "I loved your mother. I did. I swear, I did as best I could at the time, with so little life experience, and a butt load of ambition. But—"

"You love Cheryl now." He's certain, intuitive like his mom.

I glance to Gabriel and back. "I love Cher." I step into my son. "I was a kid with Vera, loved with a kid's selfish love. I hurt her. She hurt me. I carried that hurt with me for too fucking long. Your mom didn't stop me from getting married and having kids." I slap my chest. "I did. So please don't, for one second, blame my broken insides on her. I did that—I allowed it to happen. I fed it. I propagated it like a fucking farmer. All on me. You understand?"

"Yeah." His dimpled, agreeable grin eases my concerns. "You loved my mom, but not the same as you love his mom." He slaps Gabriel on the back. "You were just kids."

"Fucker." Gabriel flinches.

I step into Gabriel, placing my hand on each of their shoulders. "I love your mom, son. I think I have for a while. It just took me a minute to figure it out."

"To get out of your own way," he adds. He knows. He did the same with Frankie.

"Yeah, for damn sure." I step back, feeling like I can breathe for the first time since leaving Cher at the bakery. "I want to marry her, and I want your blessings."

"If you didn't already have my blessing, I never would have told you to figure your shit out with Mom." Gabriel hugs me hard, like he might be trying to kill me instead. "You took me in when I was a punk-ass kid. You're a father to my Angel. Grandfather to my son. You're already family, Cap, but I'd be honored to make it official with you marrying Mom."

Fuck. For a tough motherfucker, he sure can dole out the emotions. "The honor's all mine, Gabriel." I hug him tighter, then release him to check on the status of my son by blood.

Rowdy eyes me sheepishly, tight smile, clenched jaw. He dips his head and looks away. "I'm sorry things didn't work out with my mom. It would have been nice to be raised by you…" He smashes his mouth with his fist as his shoulders shake.

I pull him in, holding him, palm the back of his head, trying to give him comfort. Regret and what-ifs are a bitch. "I'm sorry I missed it too, but we're here now. I'm thankful to have any part of your life, and honored as hell to call you *Son*."

"Damn." Gabriel pats our backs, eyes glistening with emotion.

Moving back, I sniff, reining in the powerful feels before we're all blubbering idiots. "So proud of y'all."

"Fuck, Cap. Enough. We love you too," Gabriel growls, making Rowdy and me laugh.

"Yeah, yeah. I just needed to be sure you knew."

"You make it clear, Cap. You're not the most reserved person when it comes to how you feel about someone." Rowdy's gaze flashes to me. "Love you too, by the way. And I'm proud to be your son."

"Christ." I grasp their shoulders. "Love you both as sons. Always." No matter what, these two are mine.

"So, when are you going to ask her?" Gabriel swipes at his eyes.

"Soon. But…" I lock on Rowdy. "You're first."

He turns fifty shades of red before facing Gabriel. "You okay with that?"

"What? You marrying my baby sister?"

"Yeah." Rowdy stands taller, ready to take on this fight if need be.

Gabriel laughs, shaking his head. "You've no idea how much it means to see my girls happy. I never… I wasn't sure either of them would ever be. So yeah." He points at me. "Marry my mom." He flattens his hand on Rowdy's chest. "And you gave my sister more life than I ever thought possible. Marry her. Have babies." He looks between us. "Just make 'em happy." He shakes his head, dispelling all the gushiness. "Fuck. Can we be done with this? Jesus."

"Please," Rowdy groans.

"Yep." I raise my hands. "Done."

"Thank God." Gabriel starts toward the edge of the lake. "Can we talk about Cowboy and his fight?"

"Cap! Jesus, there you are." Reese comes running out the back door. "Your phone's been ringing off the hook, and there's a man on your office phone who says he needs to talk to you. It's an emergency."

"Who?" I jog to her. I left my phone on my desk in my haste to have this conversation with my boys.

"Um, Tumble Weed? Can that be right?" She hands me my phone.

"Fuck!" I touch the screen and see all the missed calls. Fuck. Fuck. Fuck. "I gotta go." I call him back, pulling my keys out of my pocket and running around the building to my truck.

"Where the fuck have you been?" Weed answers in a huff.

"What's wrong?"

"Hot." He hangs up.

"Fuck." I unlock the door, practically diving for the burner phone hidden in my center console, start the car, and call Tumble Weed back. All the while ignoring the calls and questions from Gabriel and Rowdy who have jumped in, shut and locked the doors. "Out!"

"No, whatever's going on, we're here for you," from Gabriel.

"Not leaving," from Rowdy in the back seat.

"Talk," I bite at Weed when he answers.

"The scuttle says Germain sent an ex-con to pay Mrs. Stone a visit. Have you seen her? Talked to her?"

"Jesus, fuck." I nearly swerve off the road. Gabriel grips the steering wheel right as I gain control of my senses. "I got it," I bark at him, then shoot him an apologetic glance. "Not in a few hours," I say to Weed. "I'm on my way now. How the fuck does this happen? Never mind." I already know. The criminal justice system is full of weasels dying to make a quick buck.

"About the other thing..." He's caught on I'm not alone.

"Yep."

"Tomorrow. Just after midnight. Be ready."

"Got it." I hang up and drop the burner in the cup holder. I'll have to trash it after tomorrow. I floor it to the bakery. This is not the way Cher wanted our family to find out about our new endeavor. I pray she forgives me, but given the circumstances—

"What the fuck's going on?" Gabriel grates from the passenger seat, holding on as I take a corner entirely too fast.

"Your dad sent someone to check in on Cher."

"The fuck?"

"We're going the wrong way," Rowdy chimes in.

"No. No, we're not."

Fuck! You better forgive me, Cher, for giving up your secret. And you better be fucking okay.

You hear me?

We're just getting started. I finally figured it the fuck out, got our boys onboard. Don't you fucking leave me.

CHAPTER 28

CHER

HIS GRIP TIGHTENS AFTER LETTING ME GET A few gulps of air. "Germain said you were a looker. He wasn't lying. Too bad he made me promise not to take a piece for myself." He leans closer, breathing me in.

His stench is horrendous, like rotten eggs and backed-up sewer lines. My stomach churns, and panic ratchets up a few hundred notches.

"Fuck if you don't smell good enough to eat—one broken piece at a time." He licks my cheek. "Stone's gonna be dead soon. He'd never know, right?"

Dead. Germain is going to die alright, but it won't be from cancer. It will be by my hands. The reminder clears my head. I can think instead of only fighting for air. He doesn't have me pinned against the counter.

I drop. Dead weight.

His single grip on me fails. I sucker punch him in the balls on my way down, rolling away and popping to my feet as he doubles over.

"Fucking bitch," he coughs and spits. "You're dead."

Yeah, I don't think so. I reach for the first things I spot that will inflict the most damage: a chef's knife and a cast iron skillet. Two items I brought from home this morning and hadn't put away yet.

Knife in my right hand, skillet in my left, I give him a wide berth. I should run, I'm sure. But my feet don't move away. They circle him—like he's my prey. I'm tired of being the weakling, the victim. I'm not that person anymore. I refuse to be.

I'll kill him or die trying.

Hands on his knees, he side-eyes me as I circle. "What are you doing, you crazy bitch? Germain beat you one too many times. You loco?" He groans as he straightens.

"You can leave or die." I motion to the back door. "Your choice."

"You're not as big as a minute. I could break your neck hardly trying."

"Then why didn't you?"

"Why… What the fuck? You are crazy."

"Leave. Or die."

He laughs. He doesn't believe me. It's okay. I wouldn't have believed me either, not a week or so ago. But hearing what Germain did to my sweet girl, what he *thought* he did, switched something on in my brain. I will never be the victim again. I will be friend or foe, no in-between, no other roles. I'm all out of *victim*.

Light on my feet, I bounce, like I've seen my son do so many times. Be agile. Be moving. Ready to strike. I loosen my shoulders, swing the pan, wiggle the knife.

The man in front of me stares like I'm crazy. Maybe I am. But it's put him off his game. I'm not one to miss an opportunity.

"You want me. You come and get me." I'm taunting the big sloth of a man.

He's breathing hard. He limps when he turns, keeping me face-on.

I see it, the second he readies to strike. The tic of his muscles. The decision on his face. Germain taught me well. A lesson hard-earned but welcome at this very moment.

He runs at me, growling like an angry bear, his weight forward, arms ready to pump or punch. It's two steps, slow motion, time grinding to a halt. I run to meet him and lunge but not in the way he anticipates. I slide, feet first—like I used to do in softball as a kid. I was fast. I'd nearly forgotten.

He reaches, trying to nab me, but I swing the pan, striking him in the side of the knee. The snap of ligaments is unmistakable. Right before I slide between his legs as he's on his way down, I bury the knife in his gut.

"Christ almighty!"

My head swivels to meet Cap's angry green orbs, spitting fire and rage as I spin and slam into the opposite wall, hitting the steel counter with more force than can be good for a body. Air knocked out of me. All I can do is mouth his name as dots flash in my vision and darkness ascends.

CAP

Pulling into the shopping center, I bypass the front, speed around the back, nearly side-swipe a workman taking a smoke, slam on the brakes and barely get it into park before sprinting out the door and into the back of Sugarplum's.

"What the fuck is this?" Gabriel, hot on my heels, asks with Rowdy's, "Why are we here?"

"Later," I growl. My woman's life is on the line.

Gabriel called her repeatedly on the way over. Every call went to voicemail.

Worry ices my spine, and rage spurs my focus as we rush through the back corridor, about to round the corner, when a roar fills the air. That's not my Cher.

"What the—" Gabriel's words die as the kitchen comes into view, and a man smaller than us but bigger than my Plum misses his tackle as my girl slides just out of reach, hitting him with a one-two punch of frying pan and knife.

"Christ Almighty!" I see it, but I don't believe it. I leave the dead man to Gabriel and Rowdy and dive for my girl, trying to catch her before she slams into the metal shelf in a current trajectory of head-first. "Cher!"

I don't make it. She's knocked clean out. "Cher! Fuck. Wake up, baby."

"Don't move her!" Gabriel shouts. "She could have a neck injury."

"Fuck." I pull my hands back, ready to pull her into my arms. She just got over the mild concussion and the cut on her scalp from Tom. At this rate, my woman's going to have brain damage or worse.

"Let me look." Gabriel slides in next to me.

"The guy—"

"Rowdy's got it. Guy's bleeding like a stuck pig. He's not going anywhere. The cops are on their way."

Thank God.

"Mom? Can you hear me?" Gabriel checks her pulse, runs his hands along her ribs as best he can without moving her.

"Gabriel." His eyes meet mine. "We can't tell the cops about the phone call. It's off the record. Could cause trouble down the line."

He nods. "Rowdy." He waits until my son meets his gaze. "We called, couldn't reach Mom. We panicked and flew over here from the gym." His eyes back on me. "Where are we, Cap?"

"Her bakery, Sugarplum's. We were going to tell you guys this weekend. She wanted it to be a surprise."

"I was afraid you wouldn't approve." Cher's voice, barely a whisper, pierces my heart.

"Cher." I squeeze her hand, unable to resist touching her in some way.

"Cap." She winces and tries to sit up.

"Don't move, Mom."

"Pfft." She pushes Gabriel's hands away. "I've been hit worse. Now let me up."

CHAPTER 29

CAP

"**D**AMN, THAT WAS SOMETHING. YOU WERE a fucking Minnie Mouse ninja," Rowdy says to Cher as we wait for Gabriel to pull my truck around outside the ER. He didn't get a chance to fawn over her until now.

She laughs, then groans, holding her head. She has another bump, bruising around her neck, but no concussion or lacerations this time.

I kiss her temple, holding her close. "No more ER visits, Plum." Her eyes meet mine. "I can't take it."

She pats my chest, laying her head over my heart. "Okay, Cap. No more," she placates me. I'll take it.

The police and ambulance showed up quickly. They carted the assailant off while a second set of EMTs checked out Cher and the police questioned us. Pretty routine.

The cops are following up on Cher's statement that Germain sent the guy to rough her up as a final goodbye before he died. From what I could hear, the guy was spilling his guts to the cops both verbally and literally due to the large knife wound in his belly. His injuries weren't bad enough to kill him, but he'll need surgery on his knee and stomach. Maybe he'll get sepsis and die anyway. Here's hoping. I don't need another deranged madman out there with a grudge against my woman.

Gabriel drives us to my place, all the secrets—nearly—out of the bag. Our relationship being one of them. When we pull into the driveway, Frankie is already there to take Gabriel and Rowdy home or to get their cars, up to them. But she's not who has my attention. It's the dark sedan with impenetrable tinted windows that pulls in behind us.

"Take your mom inside." I squeeze her hand before stepping out and closing the door behind me. I don't want her to follow, and I know my boys will take care of her and Frankie.

I stand behind my truck, a wall between my family and whoever's in the government-issued vehicle, arms crossed, waiting.

Just as the front door clicks closed, the back passenger side door opens, a familiar face coming into view. Daniel Marino, the District Attorney. Fucker.

"Cap, it's good to see you looking well." His gaze sweeps my house and back. "Was that No Mercy and Rowdy going in your house?"

I step closer, offering my hand. "Like you don't know it was. What the fuck?"

He smiles, shaking my hand, moving closer. "I gotta keep up appearances, Cap. Can't let my men know there's a more important man than me who lives here."

"You already got my vote, Marino. You don't need to kiss my ass."

His smile turns to concern. "I heard you got some trouble going on with Germain Stone and his ex-wife. She okay?"

"She's good." Or she will be as soon as I get her alone.

"Good. I came to offer my help. I owe you. There's no question about that. You saved my ass more times than I can ever repay. But I do need to ask you something." He motions to my house. "You think we could go in, could use a little privacy?"

Introductions complete, I kiss Cher. "Go rest. I'll be in in a minute." Then to my boys, I say, "Thanks for being there today."

"Cap, we're not going anywhere." Gabriel points to the kitchen. "I'm gonna make us some food."

Damn, sounds great. I'm starved. "I'll be back."

Daniel and I disappear down the hall into my office. "Sit." I point at the couch or the chairs in front of my desk. I'd offer him a drink, but he's fifteen years sober. Quite an accomplishment for all he's been through and achieved.

I lean on my desk, giving him my full attention.

Hands buried in his pockets, he looks up sheepishly. "I always feel like such a kid around you, Cap."

My brows shoot up. "You're older than me, Daniel."

He smirks. "Yeah, in age, but not mentality. You always had your head on straight. Took me a while to find my way."

He has no idea. "But you did. That's what matters. And look at you now, our DA. I'm proud of you."

"See, always on point. You save people, Cap. That's what you do." He hands me a slip of paper. "The guy who attacked Cheryl Stone today. The cops got a full confession out of him. Germain Stone signed over a large sum of money to him to take Cheryl Stone out. Not just beat her up."

"The fuck!"

"Yeah, had a feeling you didn't know that part." He sits on the couch. "Your shopping center is looking good. Sugarplum's is bound to be a hit. I've tasted her desserts. She doesn't get paid near enough. I'm glad she broke it off with Tom and his family. I'll be sending plenty of business her way. Let me know when you're having your grand opening. I'll come do a ribbon cutting, shake hands, serve food, whatever. She's a nice lady and deserves this chance."

Damn. "You're serious?"

"As a heart attack."

"Wait." I come to my full height. "How did you know about Cher and Tom no longer working together?"

"Caro. She told me she ran into you a few weeks back. Seems you walked in on—"

"You knew?"

He chuckles. "My wife loves her kink. She also can't keep a secret to save her life. Lucky for her, I love her kink too. Also, they're not blood-related."

Wow. Wasn't expecting that. "She begged me not to tell you."

"That was for Tom's sake and to get money out of Tom for Cher. He did deliver, didn't he?"

"He did."

"Good. If she needs more, Tom's got plenty more where that came from."

"She doesn't need a damn thing from him, except to stay away from her."

"Already handled. He knows his place. He won't be stepping out of line. But—"

"You want the video."

He nods. "It's truly not why I'm here. I was going to come to you eventually if you didn't come to me—"

I would have. I don't like keeping such secrets from friends. But I had to be sure Cher was all set first.

"—But today's events sped up my need to see you."

"Understood." I walk around my desk, turning on my laptop, and take a seat.

He walks over, fingering the name on the piece of paper he gave me. "He's taken care of." His eyes meet mine. "Seems he got in deep with some rather unsavory sorts. I hear he didn't make it out of surgery."

Christ.

"Also," he slides another piece of paper over, "Web will pick you up at this address at 11pm tomorrow night. Don't be late."

"How'd you know?" I'd only talked to Tumble Weed about this. I purposely kept Web out of it. I didn't want him or anyone else getting in trouble.

"I called Tumble Weed. The three of us worked it out. Got you covered. Seems we're having a citywide outage for the street cameras tomorrow night for a software update from 10pm till around 2am. It's mandatory. Can't be helped."

I stand, overcome. "I don't—"

"You don't need to. I heard about Vera. I'm really sorry. But I'm glad to hear about Rowdy and your daughter. I hope to meet her one day."

"Yeah, probably not with your kinky inclinations."

He laughs. "Probably for the best." He claps my shoulder. "I'm happy you've got a second chance with Cher. You've known her long enough you could have had a brood by now."

"Yeah, took me a minute."

"I'll say."

I put the only copy of the video of his wife and her brother—though apparently not by blood—on a pen drive and hand it over. "I would have told you."

"I know. Your problem was with Tom, not me. You were looking out for your woman. I'm doing the same. We're good. We'll always be good, Cap. I owe you the world. This is only a start."

After seeing him out, I join my family for food and figuring out what the hell to do about tomorrow night.

CHAPTER 30

CHER

ISINK IN FURTHER, THE HEAT OF THE BATH AND the feel of him wrapped around me enough to lull me into heavy eyelids and dreamy thoughts of nights like this forever.

He kisses my temple as he massages, drawing lazy circles across my skin. "You sure you're okay?"

"Mm-hmm." I'm perfect.

"He sent someone to kill you, Cher. We haven't talked about that. It has to be upsetting. It's like you've shut down your emotions when it comes to Germain—since the kids visited him and you found out how vile he really is."

He's not wrong. "Not shut down, redirected."

"What do you mean?"

He'll never let me go if I tell him my plan. But he may never forgive me if I don't.

I turn to face him. He helps me straddle his legs, something I could never do in the tub in my house. Also, something I've never done—take a bath with a man. It's tender and loving and incredibly intimate. His manhood nestled between us. My breasts on full display if not for being smooshed against his chest or the dissipating bubbles that lazily pop around us.

"I have to tell you something. You're not going to like it. But my mind is made—"

"You're going to see Germain."

"How?!"

"The warden is a Marine… A brother."

I cock my head, studying this man who is stoic so much of the time, yet I feel his emotions rolling off him in waves. Haven't I always seen them, felt them? It's why I was so hurt when he pulled away from me all those years ago—telling me he could only be a protector, nothing more, not a lover, barely even a friend. I was so hurt, I locked myself away for years, barely coming out for groceries, seeing no one except Gabriel and Reese. Cap still came to mow my lawn, but I never stepped out. I never brought him drinks or food. Not once. He closed the door. I locked it.

But not anymore. "You hurt me all those years ago when you said you couldn't be lovers."

He flinches. "Cher, I—"

"No, you did what you needed to do. You thought I wanted something from you. Something you couldn't give. But I only wanted a friend, James. You made me feel every bit as broken as I was. I felt unwanted, unlovable. I felt ugly."

"Christ, baby, you're none of those things. I've never seen you that way."

"I know that now. I didn't then."

"I didn't think I could love you the way you needed. I didn't want to be the *next man* who broke your heart. I thought I was offering you friendship. I was too harsh, too direct."

"You were right, though. I wasn't ready. I couldn't have been friends with you, Cap, because I was *in love* with you."

He sucks in air, his chest rising, his eyes misting over. "Say that again."

"I've been afraid nearly my whole life. The only time I'm never afraid is when I'm with you. That's not to say I don't still have issues, and sometimes they get triggered, but it's not you I fear—never you. I don't know when, but it happened somewhere between Gabriel leaving for the army and you telling me we couldn't be *more*."

He cups my cheek, his wet hand warm on my skin. "*What* happened, Cher?"

"I fell in love with you."

"Fuck." He pulls me closer. "And now?" he breathes across my mouth, his heart thundering against my chest.

"I'm more in love with you than ever."

"Fuck me." He ends the distance, his mouth consuming mine. "Fuck," he gasps, coming back for more. Deep, hungry, needful kisses. "I love you too, Cher." He holds me still, my face in his hands. "I've loved you for so fucking long and didn't even know it, until Tom hurt you. You called *me*. The way that felt… You *needed* me."

"So much," I whisper against his lips.

"I'm sorry it took me so long to figure it out. What I feel for you is new. I've never felt this much, this deep, this painfully before."

"Not even—"

"Never, baby. Only you."

He ravages my mouth till I'm moaning and begging him to fill me. Just when I think he might, he breaks our kiss, holding me back. "We need to talk about Germain, Cher. Did you tell me all of this to distract me?"

God, no. I smile, trying to fill my lungs with air. "No. I knew I needed to tell you because I didn't want any more secrets between us, but I realized that pain was something I needed to share with you too. Let you know I understood. It was something you needed to do. Neither of us was ready. I'm ready now, Cap, but I have one more thing I need to do."

"What's that?"

"Kill Germain."

CAP

"Christ Almighty, Cher. You're insane if you think I'm going to let you do that." My heart is beating so hard, I think it might break free and burrow its way into her chest to reside forever next to hers, keeping it safe.

I asked her to *need me*. Can I give her this? Silently, we get out of the tub. A towel slung around my waist, I dry her off slowly, methodically, and with great care.

Her hand over my heart, she nods, and her resolve settles around us, her words soft yet assured, "I'm not really asking, Cap. I know you can stop me physically. I'm hoping you won't. I could use your help."

She holds on to me as I lift her leg, drying off her foot, moving up her leg toward her center. Her hands are lost in my hair as I kneel before her, repeating the process with her other leg.

I wrap around her, my head on her stomach just below her breasts, holding her tight. "Taking a life is not easy, Cher. I don't want it to haunt you. Let me do this for you."

Cupping my face, running her fingers through my hair, she lifts my gaze to hers. "He haunts me now. He's in every dark corner, every shadow or quick movement in my periphery. He's every loud bang, plate drop, forgotten task, burned or cold meal. He's every scar on my body—inside and out. He's in Gabriel's scowl and need to fight. He's in Reese's fear of the dark and touch. He's my every regret and my greatest weakness." A single tear trails down her cheek. "He haunts me now, Cap, but I have to be the one to end this for us. I don't think I can do it alone. Free us from his ghost. Help me bury him."

Fuck. "Okay." I wanted to save her from this, from ending his life. But she needs closure—a murderous kind of closure—but closure all the same. I kiss her softly. "Whatever you need, Plum." Whatever she fucking needs. It's my honor, my duty, my right.

I kiss her deeper, carrying her to bed. Murder on my mind but love in my heart. She told me she loved me, has for a long time.

Finally

Finally.

Finally, I see a future worth fighting for. Funny thing is, it doesn't involve fighting at all. My life has revolved around my fighters, my business—always fighting-related. Now, it's about loving my Cher with everything I have and all my resources to give her peace and safety from her past, and seeing her dream of a bakery come to fruition.

And loving the fuck out of her.

CHAPTER 31

CAP

CONFIDENT IS HOW I'D DESCRIBE MY WOMAN AS she sits next to me all in black, sexy as fuck all the way down to her black biker boots.

We're about to commit murder, and she's giving me wood.

What the fuck's wrong with me?

"You okay?" She pins me with her gaze, placing her gloved hand on my thigh.

Before we exited my truck to get in Web's van, I handed her black nitrile gloves to hide our fingerprints. I thought of military gloves, but I want disposable and less bulky, plus I don't own a pair small enough for her perfect little hands.

I squeeze her hand, meeting her gaze. "I don't want you to regret this." I've killed before, not quite like this. Germain deserves to die. I won't regret that. Not for one moment. But she might. "You change your mind at any time, you just say the word. I'll take care of him."

"I won't change my mind."

I believe her. She's determined to put her past behind her, and that starts by ending the source of her family's pain.

I'm all in. I might have given up my own ideas of murder if he hadn't sent someone to kill her. With every breath he takes, he's a threat to my family. I won't let that stand. I pull her into my side, kiss her head and watch the world pass by as Web drives us to the prison.

Other than a crooked brow, Web didn't say a word when the two of us climbed in the back of the delivery van. Any questions he has related to Cher being here, I've already considered. He trusts me.

Tumble Weed, I'm not too sure about. I've no doubt I'll get a word or two out of him, even if Web does give him a heads-up.

When we're let through the main gate, I slip a baggie in her hand. "Put this in your boot or pocket. If anything goes wrong, you take it. When you wake up, you tell them you don't remember anything since the attack at the bakery."

She frowns at the bag containing a single pill. "What is it?"

"Your alibi."

"I'm not leaving you to take the rap."

I smile, chucking her chin. "You will, or we'll turn around now. I'm not letting him ruin another second of your life."

"I'm not letting him ruin yours either." She pushes the pill back in my hand. "I dragged you into this. It's *your* alibi."

The hell it is.

The back doors of the van open, and she's out before I can stop her or force the pill into her possession. "Stubborn woman," I groan as I climb out, pocketing the pill. I'll force it down her throat if I have to.

Tumble Weed doesn't miss what I pocketed. His gaze darts between Cher and me. "You won't need that. I've got you covered, Cap."

He steps forward, offering his hand to her. "Nice to meet you, Cheryl. I'm Tumble Weed." When her brows shoot up at his name, he just chuckles and whispers, "I'm Warden Rex Kirk, but my friends call me Weed. Cap can explain later."

With a quick nod to Web, who's staying with the van at the loading dock, Cher and I follow closely behind Tumble Weed. The prison is eerily quiet. Not a sound until we reach the hospital ward. Though Weed advised the cameras are offline for maintenance updates, Cher and I still wear black baseball caps and keep our faces down. I should have blacked out her face as an extra precaution.

When he stops at a door, he motions, letting me know this is the one. "Twenty," he whispers and unlocks the door.

We've got twenty minutes to do the deed and get out. I only need two, but my woman may need a bit more.

I pull Cher into my chest, my hand wrapped around the side of her face, whispering in the other ear, "You better not hate me for this, Plum."

She stops me from pulling away. "I love you even more for this. Thank you."

Damn, any barbed wire left around my heart just broke free. I kiss her cheek, telling her, "You stay by the door until I call you over." I wait for her agreement then push in, pulling her behind me.

CHER

The smell has me gagging the second I walk through the door. The sight of Germain in the bed is blocked for a moment as Cap moves forward. When my ex-husband comes into view, I fight the urge to cower, my pulse dancing a few beats faster. His power over me is ingrained so deeply even after all these years.

He sent someone to kill you. The reminder emboldens me. I can do this for Reese and Gabriel—and a tiny bit for me.

"Who the hell are you?" The grate of Germain's voice sends shivers down my spine. I'll never forget the edge to his voice, the distain, the devil's croak ever present.

"I'm the man who loves Cher, Gabriel, and Reese. They're mine. And you hurt what's mine." The possessive growl in Cap's voice sends goosebumps along my skin. My response to him is so different and so very wanted. Cap holds his hand out to me. "Come closer, Cher. He can't hurt you anymore."

In the dimly lit space, I can barely make out Germain's gaze as he searches the room, but his head stills when I step out of the shadows and into view. "Come by for a quick fuck before I die, Cheryl?"

"Like you could get it up, you nasty piece of shit." Ohmygod, did that come out of my mouth?

I catch Cap's smirk. I guess it did.

"Your mouth is finally as loose as your cunt, I see."

Whoomph. Cap punches him in the groin.

Germain coughs and struggles to draw in air. In his jerky movements, I notice his wrists are cuffed to the bed. Cap didn't have time to do that. Germain was already cuffed when we arrived. He can't hurt me even if he tried. He's powerless. He's helpless.

"That's your only warning. Disparage her again, and the next strike will be worse."

Germain opens his mouth to retort, but the daggers coming out of Cap's eyes keep my ex silent. They also fill me with the confidence I need.

Taking in the last sight of the man who caused me and my kids so much pain and misery, I feel sorry for him. His whole body is screaming *death*. He's so close. He's suffering—how could I end that suffering by killing him? Being reduced to this must kill Germain's ego… And that means there's something I can do that will be worse than killing him.

I step closer. "I want you to know the kids and I have a good life. We've found love, moved on from you. After tonight, you are dead to us. You think you got everything you wanted from us…"

He glares, his lips moving like he's dying to say something nasty. I'm sure he is, but Cap moving into his line of sight keeps Germain silent.

I relish my next words, "You think you raped our daughter, you didn't. It was Lola, our neighbor's kid—that doesn't make it better, but I'm thrilled to take this one thing from you that you *thought* you had taken from someone else. You're a sick fuck, Germain. Evil. I would wish I'd never met you, but I don't regret our kids—not for a second." I come to stand next to Cap, looking down on the pitiful man below me, withering away in his own filth. "No one will miss you when you die. No one will mourn your passing. You will fade out of existence like a nasty little blip."

Cap hugs me to his side. "You ready?"

The man in the bed forgotten, I'm lost in Cap's green-eyed embrace, full of love and sacrifice. I reach up, pulling his head down, kiss his jaw and whisper words in his ear meant only for him.

"You sure?" He needs confirmation.

I'm more than sure. "I'm done here."

CHAPTER 32

CAP

"CHER, I SWEAR TO GOD..." I FIST THE SHEETS, grit my teeth and pray not to come. Not fucking yet. She swirls then sucks on the tip, slowly drawing me back into her mouth. "Christ." I'm not coming like this.

The second we got home, I carried her to my bedroom with every intention of eating my fill until she couldn't see straight. The minx turned the tables on me, ravenously sucking my cock like she's trying to get the last little bit of milkshake out of the bottom of the glass with a straw. She's had her hands on me before, but this is the first time her mouth made it past my abdominals. Not complaining—at least I wasn't until now. Now I know what she's like—greedy and fucking fantastic.

"Need you," she moans around my cock, her hips dipping, looking for relief.

I pull her up my body and kiss her greedy, swollen lips till I feel her wetness coating my abdomen. "Ride or be ridden?" Choose. Quickly.

My girl shudders. I palm her ass, squeezing and separating her glorious globes, my fingers getting wet and needy. She steals another kiss before answering, "Both."

"Then get on my cock, Cher. I'm not gonna last long." She's got me too worked up.

My warrior faced down her tormentor tonight, and instead of ending his miserable existence, she pardoned him.

Not the route I would have taken or how I envisioned the night going, but I'm proud as fuck. She chose not to lose a part of her soul by taking his life. It was a gift to herself. A gift to her kids to not know or suspect we killed their father. Though, I know either of them would have loved the chance themselves. But when it comes right down to it, Gabriel and I are the only ones that know the toll of taking a life—we're the only ones who have killed. It's best it stays that way.

My eyes roll back, and we both moan when she lowers herself down my cock. So fucking wet. So fucking warm. So fucking *mine*.

Christ. She's an adrenaline rush, a stiff drink, a winning lottery ticket, a beautiful sunrise and sunset all wrapped in one tight, sinfully delicious body that holds my fucking heart. "Fuck, baby." I grip her hips, fingers splayed across her ass, urging her on as she rides me so fucking good.

She slams forward, her hands landing on my chest, clawing my pecs, her breasts pressed together between her arms, her head down, a curtain of black hair sweeping back and forth around her shoulders. Little grunts of *yes, ohmygod, feels so good* leave her lips on each thrust, a running dialogue of what I'm doing to her, when really, it's her doing it to me.

"Riding me so fucking good, Plum." I palm her tits, groaning when her pussy walls squeeze me, threatening to end the cock ride before she gets there.

Not happening.

I slide my hand down her stomach, relishing the feel of her muscles tightening under my touch and the strength in her thrusts. My woman is fit and tight all over. Baking does a body good—so fucking good. Lower, my thumb finds her clit, throwing off her rhythm.

"Gaaah!" Her gaze locks on me, her jaw clenched, frustrated at her lost timing.

"Find it, baby." I rub in circles over her clit, teasing her nipples. When she still struggles, I sit up enough to capture a nipple in my mouth and tease it properly.

She holds my head to her breasts, begging, "Please."

Her frustration grows as her urgency rises, unable to reach the release she's desperately seeking.

"I got you, baby." With little thought, I flip us over, pull her legs over mine, spread wide on my knees. Holding her lower body off the bed, I grip her hips and shove back inside. "Fuck." I was just there, but each time feels like the first time I've felt her glorious heat around my cock. Every. Fucking. Time. "Hold on," I command, burying myself in deep, pulling out then slamming home again. Hard. Fast.

The sounds of our bodies coming together fill the room. Wet slapping noises mix with my grunts and her moans. It's an erotic symphony, making me harder and her even more undone. Damn, if I don't want that on my playlist on repeat.

"Come for me, Cher. Fucking come for me." It sounds like a command. It's really a plea, 'cause I'm about to fill her up, and I really want her to find her heaven before I do.

I stretch my hand to stroke her clit with each thrust and still hold on to her hips.

"Yes!" She releases the headboard, palming her breasts before squeezing and twisting her nipples.

The sight has me roaring, ready to blow. "Cher!"

She bows off the bed, her head thrown back, her cries echoing off the walls as she finds her peak and falls the fuck over the edge, milking me, coaxing me into giving her my seed.

And I do. Thrusting through her clenching pussy, fucking tight and perfect, I fill her up. Give her all I've got and more still. So fucking much more.

One final roar, one final thrust, I collapse, barely able to breathe, twitching and throbbing inside her.

I've died.

Finally found my heaven, my peace, my forever after, and I go and die.

CHER

Warmth surrounds me, languid fingers exploring between my legs. My hips flex forward when he hits my clit. "Cap," I groggily whisper. I must have fallen asleep.

I rode him hard but couldn't find my way. He took over and brought us home. Skilled to perfection, this man.

He nibbles and sucks on my shoulder, moving up my neck, his hard body behind me, on our sides. He pushes his leg between mine, lifting it, opening me up.

"Gah," I moan when he slips inside, deep, and deeper still. "Cap."

He bites my earlobe, then sucks. "Keep saying my name, Plum. Never stop." Quick thrusts.

"Ohmygod." How does he do that? Get me going so fast. Making me press back into him, begging to feel him deeper, to feel him everywhere.

He wraps me in his arms, my breast in one hand, my mound in the other. "I love you, Cher. You hear me?"

"Yes." I hold on tight, eating up his words, taking every inch of pleasure his body is drilling into me. "Love you, my Cap."

He growls and bites my neck, rutting into me harder and faster. His entire hand is cupping my pussy, rubbing my clit, lower lips. He has to be touching his own cock. I shudder at the thought, wanting to see it. "Mirror," I moan.

"What?" He kisses my jaw when I look over my shoulder.

"I want a mirror to watch you." I flush, the heat burning my skin from the inside out.

"Fuck." He thrusts harder. "Mouth," he orders.

I turn till his mouth finds mine, possessive, dirty, and all mine. He kisses his pleasure into me as his cock drills home.

Right before I come, he breaks our kiss. "You want to watch me fucking you?"

"Yes," I admit.

"Fuck. You're perfect, Plum. So fucking perfect."

He plunders me into two orgasms before finding his own. Then he carries me to the closet where he opens the door and sets me on all fours before the full-length mirror. He runs his hands along my back, smacking my ass before kneading the sting away. His eyes meet mine in the mirror just before he slips his fingers inside me.

"Fuck, the drunk lust in your eyes and my cum dripping down your legs has me hard again. Can you take me?"

Can I? How can I not? "Please," I beg as his fingers work me, making me wet with new arousal.

"That's my Plum." He moves me till we have a side view. He works his cock between my folds, sliding in and out. My eyes lock on the motion in the mirror. He notches his tip at my entrance and slow pushes in then out a few times. When I push back, he slaps my ass. "Don't rush me."

My whimper has him leaning over me, kissing up my spine. The sight of me on all fours and him in the same position over me has me trembling with need and his gaze meeting mine in our reflection.

"I've got you, Cher." He kisses my shoulder, eyes still on me. "I've always got you."

He buries his cock inside me, so full, I nearly fall forward. Reaching behind him, he grabs some pillows I didn't even notice were on the floor. He places them under my chest. "Get comfortable. We're gonna be a while."

I wrap my arms around the pillows, my head resting to the side where I can still watch in the mirror, my ass in the air with Cap positioned behind me, gripping my hips, using them like handles.

"You alright?" He rubs my back before he pushes in again.

"Yes. Fill me, Cap. Show me all your sexy goodness."

He thrusts hard on a groan, "So fucking mine."

This sexy beast of a man drills into me with fierce ownership. His eyes never leave me, conveying with each thrust he's mine too.

I sigh and moan my approval, the sight, the feel of him over me, around me, inside me, all-consuming Cap.

He's everywhere.

He's everything.

He's my future.

He's mine.

I'm one lucky broken woman who fell for a man who loves me to pieces and puts me back together with each delicious thrust of his cock, each touch of his tender hands, and each healing kiss.

A press of his hand to my lower back as he drives forward changes the angle just enough to hit that spot that has my legs shaking and my juices flowing. When I scream his name, his growl of pleasure sends me soaring higher and his cock filling me to the brim, pumping his pleasure into me, whispering in my ear, "I want to get you pregnant."

Oh, God.

Any pleasure from two seconds ago dries up like the Sahara. Remorse and regret fill me with such pulsating sorrow, I collapse on the floor, then into myself.

He can't mean that.

He can't really—

He won't stay—

He'll leave me when he finds out the truth.

I can't—

CHAPTER 33

CAP

THE SECOND THAT WHISPERED WISH LEFT MY lips I knew it was a mistake. I'm too old. She wouldn't want kids with me. She'd never want to start over again. She just got her dream—her bakery. That's her vision of a future, not giving it up for babies and a picket fence with me. She escaped one man's prison, and I'm trying to jam her into my fantasy instead of letting her soar? I'm an asshole.

"Cher, I'm sorry. It was—"

"No, it's fine." She rolls away, bouncing to her feet like I didn't just rock her world sexually, and then knock her clean off her feet with my admission.

She reaches for her clothes and disappears into the bathroom. I take a second to straighten the room before throwing on clothes and heading downstairs to make coffee.

Whatever this conversation holds, it's gonna require caffeine. Lots of it, I fear.

Not five minutes later, Cher rushes to the front door, opening it like she didn't plan on saying goodbye.

"Where you goin', Plum?"

Her head falls forward, defeated. That *was* her plan.

Fuck. I amble over, grabbing her bag and closing the door. "I thought we were past you sneaking out on me." I'm feeling lots of things, but the only one I'm sure she hears is anger—disappointment and regret are waging war right behind it.

"I need to get to the bakery."

All I hear is she wants away from me.

"How were you planning on getting there? You don't have your car."

"Oh, I forgot."

Ask me for a ride. Don't be too proud. "Come have some coffee. We need to talk. Then I'll take you home."

I doctor her coffee, setting it and a cinnamon muffin she baked yesterday in front of her. She stares at it like I might have laced it with rat poison.

Come on, Cher, we've come so far—too far for you to shut down on me now.

We almost killed a man together last night. I think we can get past the whole poorly timed *I want to impregnate you* discussion.

I sit catty corner to her at my kitchen table, break off a piece of muffin and hold it out for her to open her mouth. "You need to eat, baby." My tone reflects the sorrow niggling in my gut.

She crumbles before my eyes. My proud, diminutive, brave woman looks up at me, chin wobbling, and drops her truth.

"I can't have more kids," she outright sobs.

I sweep her into my arms and head for the living room couch. We're gonna need a minute.

Holding her tight, I kiss her teary face. "I don't know if you mean emotionally or physically, but okay. It doesn't matter. I don't need babies. It was just an impulsive remark in the heat of the moment. I was being a complete caveman." Imagining getting her pregnant as I rutted into her from behind, the peak of male egotistical behavior. "I'm sorry, Cher."

"No, I'm sorry. I should have told you sooner—not having more kids is a deal breaker for some people. I just—"

"Never thought I'd want forever with you?"

"What?!"

I dry her tears, hoping they're gone for now but fully prepared for a new set to emerge. "I told you I wanted forever, Cher. I'm not playing here. It's you and me, Plum." I kiss her reddening nose and puffy lips. "No babies means I have more time to love on you."

"Cap."

Fuck. If she keeps saying my name like that, I'm going to be the one crying and begging her to impregnate me. I'm a total chick for my woman.

After a bit more cuddles, a quick breakfast, and new cups of coffee, I drop her home and head to the gym to get some work in. I never thought I'd be the guy who puts a woman ahead of his career, but damn if I don't want to hand the reins over to Rowdy and Gabriel and retire, keeping my Plum company as she sees her dream of owning a bakery come to fruition.

If we had kids, I could stay home and raise them, and she could work.

CHER

The air is teeming with sweet and savory smells of fresh bread, cinnamon rolls, and lots and lots of chocolate. Cakes and cupcakes are cooling, waiting to be frosted. Loaves of *Honey My Buns* wheat bread is baking, and I'm on the next step of adding the peanut butter maple layer over the oatmeal base that just came out of the oven. I just need to top it with milk chocolate chunks and butterscotch morsels and return it to the oven to finish. I've named it *Call Me Chunky* bars.

My list of menu items and cute names keeps growing. Thankfully, I'll have digitized menus upfront that can be updated and changed at any time. If something doesn't sell, it gets moved to the back burner to figure out why, and other items will be featured. I plan on having a staple of breads, cakes, and cookies always on the menu. The trick will be the quantity of each. If I'm lucky, demand will only grow.

The office furniture and tables and chairs that were to be delivered the day of the attack have miraculously appeared and been set up. I'm sure I have Cap and his lot of formidable fairies to thank. The display cases out front are clean, polished, and ready to be stuffed full of goodies. But not yet. That's next week when the staff will be training, and I have taste testers to help narrow down the grand opening menu.

Bars back in the oven, timer set, I work on icing and assembling the seven tiers of the *Death by Chocolate* cake. It's my chocolate cake with chocolate fudge frosting that Rowdy, Reese, and Cap are so fond of.

Hunger burns in my gut, and anxiousness over this morning's… *discussion* flutters around my bloodstream.

Busy hands flit this way and that, constant motion, to dissuade an idle mind from rehashing this morning. The amazing way he loves my body, drives me places I had no idea I could journey to or even wanted to visit. Now, I greedily want it all—even the kid part that I know can never be.

I was ready to leave him. Let him go to find another woman who could give him a child—his child.

A sorrowful moan builds in my belly and bursts in the air for the lost opportunity of giving Cap his own baby to raise from infancy. He has more grown *kids* than he could possibly need to fill that hole in his heart, but he missed out on raising his blood, Rowdy and Taylor.

I ache to be the one to give him that. If only I could.

I thought he didn't want that. But he said… What if he can't be happy without a baby? Now that he knows he's a father, what if that's an experience he needs? How can I stop him from having that?

The doctor told me I was done after having Reese. I never questioned it, thought to find out why. I was thankful. I'm ashamed about that now, but then, I was so very thankful not to bring another child into our house under the watchful eye and abusive touch of Germain. It *was* a blessing.

Now, it feels like a curse. A remnant of the wreckage Germain left in his wake. Like I need another reminder.

An hour or so later, when Cap walks through the back door, he finds me sitting at one of my stainless-steel workbenches, surrounded by my day's accomplishments, pad and paper in front of me, staring into nothingness. My saddened heart bounces with excitement as if he's the cure for my barrenness. Does it bother him?

He frowns. My pasted-on smile's not fooling him for a second. "Are you still upset about this morning?"

No *hello*, he just jumps right to it, stealing my breath and any hope of hiding behind a myriad of mistruths.

"Cher." He palms my cheek, leaning in until his forehead rests on mine. "I don't care about babies. I want you. We have five kids between us—it's enough. I swear."

Cap and I went from strangers to acquaintances, to a nearly friends, to rejection, then avoidance, truly friends, to finally falling head over hills in love. The journey took twelve years, yet it feels like he's seeing me, touching me for the first time—and *still* he pierces my heart with his perceptive eyes, perfect words, and possessive touch.

I latch on to him, close my eyes and take in his delicious scent mixed with the sweetness of the bakery. "How do you know?"

"I'm a highly trained operative," he teases, kisses my nose and tilts my face to his. "I want to talk about this further, but I came to give you some time-sensitive news." His hand flexes on my neck. "It really can't wait."

"Sounds ominous."

He pulls a stool around and sits with his legs bracketing mine. "I don't know how you'll react."

The softness in his eyes has my hand landing over his heart, its smooth rhythm easing me even though it's obvious he's worried. "Just tell me."

"Germain is dead."

"Wha…" I pop off the stool and stumble backwards, righting myself before Cap grasps my shoulders. "When?"

"Weed says they found him a few hours ago. He called as soon as he could. It looks like a heart attack."

I nod, biting my lip as he continues, "He removed his leads so the machines didn't go off."

He didn't want to be saved.

Would they have tried to save him?

"Cher!" Cap catches me as my legs give out.

"It's over," I sob. He can't hurt us anymore. I feel lighter and heavy all at the same time. He's gone. He's been absent from our lives for so long, but knowing he will never touch our lives again… is everything.

James holds me tightly, his mouth pressed to my temple. "It is. Whatever fears you still hold, let them go, baby. He's no more. Be free."

Through my sobs, I manage one word that spurs him into motion, "Reese."

CHAPTER 34

CAP

I DON'T BEGRUDGE CHER FOR BEING UPSET OVER Germain's death. It's not about him dying. It's about his mark on her life, the devil over her shoulder, looming presence, permanent stain that she and her kids lived through, survived. The pain he caused them is unforgivable, and yet she granted him leniency when we didn't kill him last night.

Mercy he did not deserve.

Mercy he never showed his family.

While Cher collected her belonging and boxed up more desserts than we could ever eat, I called Gabriel and Rowdy. I didn't give details, just told them to meet at Rowdy and Reese's. No choice of location either. I did that for Reese. She'll be more comfortable at home. Granted she just moved in with Rowdy, but it's her home now, and if she reacts anything like her mother, she's gonna need the privacy and comfort of home and family.

All eyes are on us when we walk in the door with arms full of sweets. It looks like we're bringing a party. We're not.

Reese's gaze ping-pongs between her mom and me. She doesn't know we're together. Or she's not sure. I thought Rowdy would have told her by now. I guess he's leaving that up to us. Like me, he's unsure how to approach the loosely strung mother-daughter relationship in which we find ourselves at opposite ends of the pendulum. Not opponents, though— never that—just supporting our woman in navigating the path to rebuild the road between them.

Though, I'm not sure there ever was a road to begin with.

Food dropped in the kitchen, I hold Cher's hand as we follow Gabriel, Frankie, Rowdy, and Reese into the living room. They sit, each man with his woman on his lap, protective arm around her back, the other slung over her lap, resting on her thighs—ready to hold, ready to love, ready to support at a moment's notice.

Cher holds me back from sitting, so I stand at her side, resting my hand on her back, keeping her close, giving her strength. She asked me to let her tell them. I'll give her space to find her voice, unless she can't. Then I'll proudly step in, giving up the news her kids need to hear from a place of love, not hate.

"Mom," Gabriel breaks the silence, "what's going on?"

As Cher leans into me, I grip her hip and watch the faces of her children when she says with respect and even a little sadness, "Your father died today."

"About fucking time," Gabriel rasps. "Good fucking riddance."

"Kitten." Rowdy cups Reese's neck, bringing her face to his.

She's shaking. I recognize the reaction, her body ready to release a lifetime of suffering and repressed emotions, hopefully not more than Rowdy is prepared to handle. But they're not alone. Never alone.

Before her first cry takes flight, Cher is there, plastering herself to Reese's back. "I'm so sorry, Reese, for what he did. For what you had to endure. Both of you." She reaches for Gabriel, who's moved himself and

Frankie beside Rowdy and Reese. Gabriel holds Cher's hand while hugging Frankie and leaning into Rowdy and Reese.

I bracket the other end, holding my woman as she breaks my heart with each admission.

"I was weak," Cher admits, talking to the back of her daughter's head, currently buried in my son's neck. "I didn't know any better. But once I did, I was too scared to leave him. I don't expect either of you to forgive me. I just want you to know I'm sorry. I'll do anything to make it right, whether it's being more present or less present in your lives. I don't deserve a second chance, but I'd sure love one."

There are more sniffles going around than I can tell who's crying, not that it matters. There's no judgment, only love and forgiveness, I pray.

The sight would make Germain sick, which only makes me happier to be a part of this remarkable family by choice, family by blood, and maybe family by marriage—if I'm lucky.

CHER

"We don't blame you, Mom." Gabriel drags me into a hug, squashing me in next to Frankie. "You were surviving the best you could. You were only a kid when you had me." He chucks my chin. "We don't blame you. You feel me?"

I hitch a sobbing breath and nod my understanding. He many not blame me, but—

"You couldn't fight him, Mom." Reese's hand finds mine. "I was there. I know what he was like. He'd threaten to hurt me to keep you compliant. He'd threaten and hurt you to keep me compliant. He was a cruel man, who deserved so much worse than he got."

He did all of that and worse. Who knows what he was into after

Gabriel kicked him out of our lives? I pray Germain is in hell as we speak, paying the price for his sins.

Cap passes out tissues, then pulls me into his lap, whispering into my neck, "So fucking proud of you."

I hold on, not letting go, until my stomach growls entirely too loudly, breaking the silence and sending everyone into a fit of laughter.

"We have chili and cornbread," Reese offers.

I smile, loving the idea of her cooking, maybe the only gift I gave my children worth being proud of. "We brought desserts."

Reese smiles but cocks a brow. "When were you going to tell me about the bakery?" She points between Cap and me. "And about this. When were you going to tell us about you two—"

"Getting married," Cap says with such certainty I only stare, dumfounded. He kisses my nose. "Marry me, Cher. Be mine, for always."

"Ohmygod!" Reese screeches. "My mom is marrying my boss."

"Your mom is marrying my dad. Maybe it could be a double wedding, Kitten." Rowdy waggles his eyebrows, making her giggle. Such a sweet sound.

"Cool your jets, Shadow. I just moved in. Let a girl breathe."

He grumbles his discontent but follows her to the kitchen, Gabriel and Frankie in tow.

Warm lips find the hollow of my neck. "You didn't answer me, Plum."

I lock on to him. "You're serious? You want my broken ass?"

He scowls but softens when I kiss his all-too-kissable mouth. "It just means you have more pieces to love, Cher. Broken or not, marry me. Say *yes*."

"Yes." The word barely leaves my mouth before his is on mine, devouring, eating and lapping at me like I'm his next meal. I shudder at the thought. Chili, dessert, then me. *Yes, please.*

"Love you, Cher."

"Love you so much, Cap."

He growls, taking my mouth for a ride that ends all too soon when

Gabriel barks from the kitchen alcove, "Quit mauling my mom and come eat."

"We have to wait until after Rowdy and Reese, though," I whisper, knowing Rowdy plans on whisking my daughter away soon.

"One week." He lifts us off the couch. "I give you one week after their wedding."

"I only need a day, Cap."

"Fuck, Plum." His forehead rests against mine. "Can we go home now?"

"Food first."

"I could eat my fill of you." His graveled tone sends chills up my spine. "Promise?"

"Fuck, yes, gladly." He nibbles my ear. "Two hours, Plum, then I'm fucking you wherever we are."

"Home. We'll definitely be home by then."

"Oh, and you're moving in with me. Starting tomorrow." He palms my ass as we walk to the kitchen.

"I am?" Another wave of chills. My man all possessive and barky does something to me.

Makes me feel wanted.

Makes me feel seen.

Makes me feel loved and cherished.

"Yep, I live closer to the bakery, closer to our family."

I love that he calls them *our* family. Cap has a heart of gold. He never forgot how to love. He just forgot he was lovable in return. "I'm going to love you hard, Cap."

"I'm counting on it, Cher. Love me so fucking hard, baby."

THE END

EPILOGUE

CHER

TWO MONTHS LATER:

THE BAKERY IS BOOMING, THOUGH WE'VE ONLY been open a few weeks. We took some time off for Reese and Rowdy's wedding, then our own. We did wait a day. One. We got married the next morning, right on the beach with all our family surrounding us in a circle. Informal and perfect.

Reese and Rowdy swore they didn't mind. They married in the little island chapel the day before, then graced us with their presence, even though it was early and only a few hours into their honeymoon. Sharing that with my daughter felt like a new start, a rebirth.

They flew off to another island for their honeymoon. We had a handful of days on the Caribbean paradise where we were married before flying home via Texas. The guys had an errand to run—something about

Rowdy's older brother—and we needed to drop off Rowdy's "father," Barrett, and sister, Taylor.

It was an interesting trip. Barrett and Cap barely said two words to each other but were civil for our kids' sake. Taylor still doesn't know Cap is her and Rowdy's father by blood, but I did catch her eyeing him and Rowdy a time or two like she was trying to figure out a puzzle. I imagine she'll figure it out before Barrett gets around to telling her. I know Rowdy and Cap don't like keeping their connection a secret from her. I don't blame them. I was tempted to tell her myself more than once.

I want to see my man happy with all his children around him. She would complete the picture. It can't happen soon enough.

"You ready?" My husband kisses my neck, warming my back with his huge body.

"You don't have to go with me. It's nothing, I'm sure."

"Then we'll be sure together." He gives my shoulders a quick squeeze, a peck on my head, and grabs our travel mugs of coffee for the road.

It's a fifteen-minute drive, a short wait, vitals taken, urine sample deposited, and another wait as Cap holds my hands, standing between my legs as I sit on the exam table. I yawn and consider laying my head on his chest for a quick power nap. I've heard of them. I've just never tried them. Sounds like a good thing to take up.

My early mornings when I baked at home didn't take it out of me like these early mornings at the bakery do. I've hired two women from the local women's shelter. They both have baking experience, one more than the other, but both with gracious attitudes and willingness to learn and share their experience. We're learning together, figuring out what works.

I have a few college kids who work up front, but my biggest surprise of all was Jess "Mustang" Riley, one of Cap's fighters. He comes in a few hours every day, early, and does the breads and cinnamon rolls, and any heavy lifting and restocking needed. He's been heaven-sent. He used to bake with his grandmother. He has a natural touch, and his big strong hands are perfect for kneading and rolling out dough. He's quiet, polite, and a hard worker. I wish I had him full-time.

The guys gave him a hard time until they tasted his bread and cinnamon rolls that rival mine and Gabriel's. Now, they come by regularly to get their fix. I'm trying out a few healthier alternatives to help them with their training instead of hindering it.

"You're thinking too hard, Plum." Cap's massive paws massage the back of my neck and head.

"I'll give you a day to stop that," I groan, sinking into his touch.

He chuckles and kisses my brow. "I'll do it every day for the rest of my life, Wife."

My response dies when there's a knock on the door.

"Come in," Cap answers, turning to face the doctor as he enters, blocking me from view. Protective much?

"Oh… Uh, sorry. I didn't expect to see—"

"I'm James Durant. Cheryl's husband."

"It's nice to meet you, Mr. Durant. I'm Dr. Morgan. I've been Cheryl's doctor for, well, a long time."

Cap's arm moves. I assume they're shaking hands, but since I can only see Cap's back, I can't be one hundred percent sure. Such men. I clear my throat in case they forgot I'm the reason we're here.

"Shit, sorry, Cher." Cap moves to the side, allowing me to see Dr. Morgan for myself.

"Hey, Doc."

"Hi, Cheryl." He shakes my hand. "I hear you're feeling a bit rundown."

"Yeah, I opened a bakery, and I guess it's taking its toll—the early hours."

His smile spans ear to ear. "My wife has been bringing home your treats for years. I'm happy to hear you've finally opened up your own shop. I'll have to stop by on Saturday, bring the grandkid, check it out."

"That'd be nice."

He picks up his laptop, screws his lips to the side. "So…" He eyes Cap, then me. "Do you want privacy?"

I nearly laugh. If I did, could I get Cap to leave the room now that the doctor asked like that? He obviously has news to share, though I'm not sure what it could be since he hasn't even taken blood or looked me over. "No, I want James here."

Cap moves to my side, his hand encasing mine.

"Well, it's not just the bakery making you tired, though I'm sure it's a lot of hard work. You might need to give yourself a bit of a break for the foreseeable future."

My husband stiffens. I frown. "Why's that?"

I can't afford to ease up. I have a new business to run.

"You're pregnant. I'd say about twelve weeks based on the date of your last period."

"What?!" I nearly come off the table before a large arm pulls me into an even harder body.

"Pregnant," Cap rasps. The awe and hope in his voice have my heart aching.

"You said I can't have more kids," I don't mean for it to sound so accusatory, but well, he did.

Embarrassed and fidgety is the best way to describe Doc at the moment. "Actually, Germain told you you couldn't have more kids. I just didn't correct him. I'm sorry about that, Cheryl." His gaze flits to my husband and back. "At the time, Mr. Stone was rather persuasive in his insistence you believe you couldn't. When, in fact, he had a vasectomy before Reese was born."

"Oh my God, that… that—"

"Asshole," Cap says for me.

"Yes. That."

"I don't disagree. Based on your history with Mr. Stone, it seemed like not having more kids with him was a good thing."

"Agreed." I'm not barren. I'm pregnant. Jesus. "Cap?"

I find him already gazing at me with such light in his eyes and a goofy ole dimpled grin. "I got you pregnant. Three months ago."

"Gloat much?"

His smile only grows. "Damn, Plum, you've given me so much. But this?" He looks to the doctor. "Can we be sure everything is okay—with the baby?"

Baby. I'm having a baby.

We're having a baby.

CAP

EIGHT MONTHS LATER

Coffees in hand, I saunter into our bedroom and still at the sight of my wife breastfeeding our twin boys. I don't know how she does it. It's called a football hold. She gets one latched, then the other, then holds their little heads, securing them in place. My woman is a regular milk factory. But the hungry buggers will take a bottle from me before they fall into a milk coma and sleep for few more hours.

This is our morning routine. For now, anyway. Jess has been a life saver at Sugarplum's. He got injured before the twins were born. He's healed enough to be in physical therapy with Frankie and run the bakery until Cher and I figure out our next steps.

Looks like they'll be coming to work with me. Well, to the daycare I had built onto the back of the Black Ops MMA Gym. Never seen a MMA gym with a nursery, but I don't give a fuck. I needed a place for my kids and my grandkids. Ox is the only one there currently, but mine will be there starting next week, and Reese is five months pregnant, so my daughter's kids will be there before long.

I didn't get to raise Rowdy and Taylor; seeing my twins like this so young is bittersweet. Though I didn't have a choice, I feel like I'm cheating on my firstborns by giving my new babies the love my older kids never got. None of us chose this path. But as I look at my wife, the *could have beens* are outdone by the *what is*. And the *what is* is staring me in the face. I'm grateful for where life has taken me—given me—a second chance, and more importantly a full family to love and protect—some by blood—all by choice.

I see a lot of babies in our future, not just mine, or mine by blood or marriage, but mine because they belong to my family by choice. Gabriel, Rowdy, and I won't be the last to find the woman they want a forever kind of thing with. I suspect Jonah and Cowboy will be next. Others will fall too. I'll make sure of it.

No man is an island. The bigger they are—or think they are—the harder they fall.

I fell hard, and I'm perfectly content to be so in love with my Plum it hurts. I've no doubt Gabriel and Rowdy feel the same.

The rest of the guys, their time is coming.

"You holding that coffee for ransom, handsome?" Cher smiles at me across the room where I'm still frozen in awe.

"Sorry, Plum." *Just busy loving you from afar.* "Bottles are warming." I sit on the side of the bed, leaning over my brood. "I swear they're bigger than they were yesterday."

I kiss each of their heads, garnering a slap on the face from Cade. I chuckle and kiss his meaty paw. "Good shot, champ." He blinks at me, sucking hard on his momma's breast. "I don't blame you. I wouldn't let go either."

I lean over, catching Wade's gaze. "What about you, little man? You got a shot for your old pop?" His hand shoots up, but instead of slapping my cheek, he just holds it there, steady, his green eyes scanning my face, blinking, then smiling, his tongue holding on to his momma's nipple for dear life. "Don't let it go. 'Cause once you do, it's mine." His lips close around his food source, sucking hard. He gets me, my intuitive little man.

Cher runs her fingers through my hair. "Miss you."

"Not for long." I kiss her mouth. "Gonna fuck you long and deep once I get these two to bed." My little cock blockers.

Thirty minutes and one orgasm down—her, not me—I'm drilling in deep in front of the three-way mirror I had installed right after I discovered my woman likes to watch. And watch she does. Her milk-laden tits bounce as I fuck her sideways. She's on her side, her leg hiked up on my shoulder, her perfect pussy on display for me and her to watch my cock drill home time and time again.

"So fucking good, Plum." Jesus, all I can think about is getting her pregnant each time I'm buried in her sweet heat.

She's going to kill me if I do. She doesn't want any more. Me, I want a baker's dozen.

"Stop that, Cap. I know that look."

"What look?"

"The one that says you can't wait to get me pregnant again."

"Fuck." I thrust and hold, swiveling, making her tremble. "If I wasn't before, I am now. Just one more, Cher. Our boys need a sister to look after, learn how to be protectors, become men of character by watching out for their sister."

"Ohmygod," my woman groans and clamps down on me so good. She grabs her breast. "I'm leaking."

Fuck. Love it when I make her milk let down. Her instinct to nourish, feed so strong. "I got you." When I urge her hand off one breast, milk shoots out. I latch on and suck.

Never thought breastmilk was a turn on before my Cher, but fuck if I don't get harder, push deeper, eating up her cries of pleasure. I move on to the next, her more sensitive nipple, making her come after only a few sucks and a flick of my tongue.

"Fuck, my sexy wife, gonna come so hard. Fill you up."

I rub her clit. Her back bows as she continues to come. "Give me a baby, Cap."

"Christalmightycher!" I drill in, giving her everything I have, pumping through full body quakes. She didn't mean it, but fuck if I'm not still hard at the idea.

"Love you, my husband."

Yep, still so hard for her. "Love you. Thank you for loving me, for needing me, Cher." My eyes mist over, my sweet seductress blurring before me.

She captures my face, holding me, nose to nose, running her thumbs under my eyes. "Love you so much, Cap. You loved my broken pieces whole."

Fuck. Me.

She said she was going to love me hard. She didn't lie.

She loves me hard as fuck, and I love her right back, just as hard, every glorious inch of her, inside and out.

She gave me love. She gave me kids, and fuck if she's not going to give me another one. I just know it. I feel it. It's gonna be a girl. A little sister for Cade, Wade, Rowdy, and Taylor. She'll be strong like my Frankie, brave like my Reese, and sugar-sweet like my Plum.

WHAT'S NEXT?

COWBOY's story is next.

Landry "Cowboy" Pierce fell hard for his best friend's sister. He didn't know it was his boss's daughter until he was in deep, too late to stop this runaway train.
Will he reach his destination with his Texas girl, or will she derail this train?

Add COWBOY to your TBR.
https://smarturl.it/COWBOY_TBR

Join my mailing list to stay up to date on COWBOY's release details, other book news, promotions, and all the happenings.

BONUS SCENES

Want more CAP and CHER?

Join my mailing list to receive exclusive BONUS Scenes for
CAP and CHER.
https://dl.bookfunnel.com/iustj6fa5c

Bonus Scenes are only available for newsletter subscribers.

DID YOU ENJOY THIS BOOK?

This is a dream for me to be able to share my love of writing with you. If you liked my story, please consider leaving a review on the retailer's site where you purchased this book and on Goodreads.

Personal recommendations to your friends and loved ones are a great compliment too. Please share, follow, join my newsletter, and help spread the word—let everyone know how much you loved Cap and Cher's story.

AUTHOR'S NOTE

I didn't know where Cap and Cher's story would take me. I'll be honest, coming out of NO MERCY and ROWDY books, I didn't particularly like Cher. I couldn't relate to a woman who let her kids, Gabriel and Reese, be victimized by their father. I hated Germain—that I had no problem with. He got off easy in my opinion.

But Cher. She was a whole other story. I'm thankful she was open and vulnerable enough to let me in—let me walk in her shoes, so to speak. Now I love her. I feel her pain and where she was coming from. I loved how her mouth ran away with itself in Cap's presence. I love how he loved her hard and didn't treat her with kid gloves, but loved her enough to be happy, sad, and mad with her—all without fear of physical abuse. They both learned the broken have more pieces to love, but together they are whole.

Cap. I love that man. I have since the first time he popped in my head. I love how he loves his misfit family, broken in so many different ways. Cap loves hard, but he didn't feel worthy of love in return. Cher showed him how it's done. Love her more for that too.

On a serious note: This is a tough subject matter. I tried my best to be honest to the characters and fair to the content, taking liberties where it was needed for the story's sake. But please, if this is you, don't suffer in silence. Reach out. There is someone, somewhere willing to help you. Whatever the abuser is telling you, it's a lie. Don't believe it. Leave. Get out. Get help. And if you have kids, love them until they're sick of your kisses and doting ways. Love yourself and your kids more than you fear the unknown if that's all that's keeping you there.

There's more Black Ops MMA Men coming. Subscribe to my newsletter to stay up to date!

ACKNOWLEDGMENTS

Thank you to my husband and kids for your endless support and encouragement. For celebrating the highs and loving me through the lows. You are my heart... my everything.

To my entire family, thank you for supporting my dream, for reading, except the guys (it's okay, I understand). Always remember it's imaginary. I'm not writing about my life. I'm not a male MMA fighter, just like it's not my sex life I'm depicting. It's called pretend. Stop telling everyone I write about sex. I write about love. Sex is just a part of that amazing love. Deal. Ha!

To the authoring community, bloggers, bookstagrammers, and readers who support me and my books—thank you, thank you, thank you. You are the bomb! Seriously. You rock!

To my editors, Tamara and Krista, thank you for making me look like I know what I'm doing—you know the truth. Tamara, thank you for your extra touch in keeping me honest to the sensitive topic of abuse. I'm not perfect, but I try... you make it better.

To my Divas (Facebook Reading Group), thank you for every encouraging word, post, gif, and demand to see CAP's story. Your love of reading and your love of the entire Black Ops gang is what drives me to write the next story and pray, pray, you aren't disappointed. Now, go shout your love for CAPTAIN (NO MERCY and ROWDY) from the rooftops!

If you're reading this right now, thank you from the bottom of my heart.

Keep reading. I'll keep writing.

Thank you for taking this journey with me.
XOXO, Dana

ABOUT THE AUTHOR

D.M. Davis is a Contemporary and New Adult Romance Author.

She is a Texas native, wife, and mother. Her background is Project Management, technical writing, and application development. D.M. has been a lifelong reader and wrote poetry in her early life, but has found her true passion in writing about love and the intricate relationships between men and women.

She writes of broken hearts and second chances, of dreamers looking for more than they have and daring to reach for it.

D.M. believes it is never too late to make a change in your own life, to become the person you always wanted to be, but were afraid you were not worth the effort.

You are worth it. Take a chance on you. You never know what's possible if you don't try. Believe in yourself as you believe in others, and see what life has to offer.

Please visit her website, dmckdavis.com, for more details, and keep in touch by signing up for her newsletter, and joining her on Facebook, Reader Group, Twitter, and Instagram.

JOIN MY READER GROUP

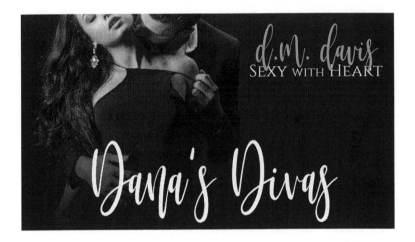

www.facebook.com/groups/dmdavisreadergroup

STALK ME

Visit www.dmckdavis.com for more details about my books.

Keep in touch by signing up for my Newsletter.

Connect on social media:
Facebook: www.facebook.com/dmdavisauthor
Instagram: www.instagram.com/dmdavisauthor
Twitter: twitter.com/dmdavisauthor
Reader's Group: www.facebook.com/groups/dmdavisreadergroup

Follow me:
BookBub: www.bookbub.com/authors/d-m-davis
Goodreads: www.goodreads.com/dmckdavis

SEXY WITH HEART
CONTEMPORARY & NEW ADULT ROMANCE AUTHOR

ADDITIONAL BOOKS BY
D.M. DAVIS

Until You Series
Book 1 - Until You Set Me Free
Book 2 - Until You Are Mine
Book 3 - Until You Say I Do
Book 4 - Until You Believe

Finding Grace Series
Book 1 - The Road to Redemption
Book 2 - The Price of Atonement

Black Ops MMA Series
Book 1 - No Mercy
Book 2 - Rowdy
Book 3 - Captain
Book 4 - Cowboy

Standalones
Warm Me Softly

www.dmckdavis.com

Printed in Great Britain
by Amazon